MYTH
CONCEPTIONS

Robert Asprin

A Legend Book

Published by Arrow Books Limited
20 Vauxhall Bridge Road, London SW1V 2SA

An imprint of Random House UK Limited

London Melbourne Sydney Auckland
Johannesburg and agencies throughout
the world

First published in 1980 by the Donning Company/
Publishers Inc.

Legend edition 1990

3 5 7 9 10 8 6 4

Printed and bound in Great Britain by
Cox & Wyman Ltd, Reading, Berkshire

ISBN 0 09 962760 4

Chapter One:

"Life is a series of rude awakenings."
— R. V. WINKLE

OF all the various unpleasant ways to be aroused from a sound sleep, one of the worst is the noise of a dragon and a unicorn playing tag.

I pried one eye open and blearily tried to focus on the room. A chair toppled noisily to the floor, convincing me the blurred images my mind was receiving were due at least in part to the irregular vibrations coming from the floor and walls. One without my vast storehouse of knowledge (hard won and painfully endured) might be inclined to blame the pandemonium on an earthquake. I didn't. The logic behind this conclusion was simple. Earthquakes were extremely uncommon in this area. A dragon and a unicorn playing tag wasn't.

It was starting out as an ordinary day . . . that is, ordinary if you're a junior magician apprenticed to a demon.

If I had been able to predict the future with any

degree of accuracy and thus forsee the events to come, I probably would have stayed in bed. I mean, fighting has never been my forte, and the idea of taking on a whole army . . . but I'm getting ahead of myself.

The thud that aroused me shook the building, accompanied by the crash of various dirty dishes shattering on the floor. The second thud was even more spectacular.

I considered doing something. I considered going back to sleep. Then I remembered my mentor's condition when he had gone to bed the night before.

That woke me up fast. The only thing nastier than a demon from Perv is a demon from Perv with a hangover.

I was on my feet and headed for the door in a flash. (My agility was a tribute more to my fear rather than to any inborn talent.) Wrenching the door open, I thrust my head outside and surveyed the terrain. The grounds outside the inn seemed normal. The weeds were totally out of hand, more than chest high in places. Something would have to be done about them someday, but my mentor didn't seem to mind their riotous growth, and since I was the logical candidate to cut them if I raised the point, I decided once again to keep silent on the subject.

Instead, I studied the various flattened patches and newly torn paths in the overgrowth, trying to determine the location or at least the direction of my quarries' movement. I had almost convinced myself that the silence was at least semipermanent and it would be all right to go back to sleep, when the ground began to tremble again. I sighed and shakily drew myself up to my full height, what there was of it, and prepared to meet the onslaught.

The unicorn was the first to come into view, great clumps of dirt flying from beneath his hooves as he ducked around the corner of the inn on my right.

"Buttercup!" I shouted in my most authoritative tone.

A split second later I had to jump back into the shelter of the doorway to avoid being trampled by the speeding beast. Though a bit miffed at his disobedience, I didn't really blame him. He had a dragon chasing him, and dragons are not notoriously agile when it comes to quick stops.

As if acting on a cue from my thoughts, the dragon burst into view. To be accurate, he didn't really burst, he thudded, shaking the inn as he rebounded off the corner. As I said, dragons are not notoriously agile.

"Gleep!" I shouted. "Stop it this instant!"

He responded by taking an affectionate swipe at me with his tail as he bounded past. Fortunately for me, the gesture went wide of its mark, hitting the inn with another jarring thud instead.

So much for my most authoritative tone. If our two faithful charges were any more obedient, I'd be lucky to escape with my life. Still I had to stop them. Whoever came up with the immortal quote about waking sleeping dragons had obviously never had to contend with a sleeping demon.

I studied the two of them chasing each other through the weeds for a few moments, then decided to handle this the easy way. Closing my eyes, I envisioned both of them, the dragon and the unicorn. Then I superimposed the image of the dragon over that of the unicorn, fleshed it out with a few strokes of my mental paintbrush, then opened my eyes.

To my eyes, the scene was the same, a dragon and

a unicorn confronting each other in a field of weeds.
But, of course, I had cast the spell, so naturally I
wouldn't be taken in. Its true effect could be read in
Gleep's reaction.

He cocked his head and peered at Buttercup, first
from this angle, then that, stretching his long serpentine neck to its limits. Then he swiveled his head until
he was looking backward and repeated the process,
scanning the surrounding weeds. Then he looked at
Buttercup again.

To his eyes, his playmate had suddenly disappeared, to be replaced by another dragon. It was all
very confusing, and he wanted his playmate back.

In my pet's defense, when I speak of his lack of
agility, both physically and mentally, I don't mean to
imply he is either clumsy or stupid. He's young,
which also accounts for his mere ten-foot length and
half-formed wings. I fully expect that when he ma-
tures—in another four or five hundred years—he will
be very deft and wise, which is more than I can say
for myself. In the unlikely event I should live that
long, all I'll be is old.

"Gleep?"

The dragon was looking at me now. Having
stretched his limited mental abilities to their utmost,
he turned to me to correct the situation or at least
provide an explanation. As the perpetrator of the
situation causing his distress, I felt horribly guilty.
For a moment, I wavered on the brink of restoring
Buttercup's normal appearance.

"If you're *quite* sure you're making enough
noise. . . ."

I winced at the deep, sarcastic tones booming close
behind me. All my efforts were for naught. Aahz was
awake.

I assumed my best hangdog attitude and turned to face him.

Needless to say, he looked terrible.

If, perchance, you think a demon covered with green scales already looks terrible, you've never encountered one with a hangover. The normal gold flecks in his yellow eyes were now copper, accented by a throbbing network of orange veins. His lips were drawn back in a painful grimace which exposed even more of his pointed teeth than his frightening, *reassuring* smile. Looming there, his fists clenched on his hips, he presented a picture terrifying enough to make a spider-bear faint.

I wasn't frightened, however. I had been with Aahz for over a year now, and knew his bark was worse than his bite. Then again, he had never bitten me.

"Gee, Aahz," I said, digging a small hole with my toe. "You're always telling me if I can't sleep through anything, I'm not really tired."

He ignored the barb, as he so frequently does when I catch him on his own quotes. Instead he squinted over my shoulder at the scene outside.

"Kid," he said. "Tell me you're practicing. Tell me you haven't really scrounged up another stupid dragon to make our lives miserable."

"I'm practicing!" I hastened to reassure him.

To prove the point, I quickly restored Buttercup's normal appearance.

"Gleep!" said Gleep happily, and the two of them were off again.

"Really, Aahz," I said innocently to head off his next caustic remark. "Where would I find another dragon in this dimension?"

"If there was one to be found here on Klah, you'd

find it," he snarled. "As I recall, you didn't have that much trouble finding this one the first time I turned my back on you. Apprentices!"

He turned and retreated out of the sunlight into the dim interior of the inn.

"If I recall," I commented, following him, "that was at the Bazaar on Deva. I couldn't get another dragon there because you won't teach me how to travel through the dimensions."

"Get off my case, kid!" he moaned. "We've been over it a thousand times. Dimension traveling is dangerous. Look at me! Stranded without my powers in a back-assward dimension like Klah, where the lifestyle is barbaric and the food is disgusting."

"You lost your powers because Garkin laced his special effects cauldron with that joke powder and then got killed before he could give you the antidote," I pointed out.

"Watch out how you talk about your old teacher," Aahz warned. "The old slime-monger was inclined to get carried away with practical jokes once in a while, true. But he was a master magician . . . and a friend of mine. If he wasn't, I wouldn't have saddled myself with his mouthy apprentice," he finished, giving me a meaningful look.

"I'm sorry, Aahz," I apologized. "It's just that I—"

"Look, kid," he interrupted wearily, "if I had my powers—which I don't—and if you were ready to learn dimension hopping—which you aren't—we could give it a try. Then, if you miscalculated and dumped us into the wrong dimension, I could get our tails out before anything bad happened. As things stand, trying to teach you dimension hopping would be more dangerous than playing Russian roulette."

"What's russian?" I asked.

The inn shook as Gleep missed the corner turn again.

"When are you going to teach your stupid dragon to play on the other side of the road?" Aahz snarled, craning his neck to glare out a window.

"I'm working on it, Aahz," I insisted soothingly. "Remember, it took me almost a whole year to housebreak him."

"Don't remind me," Aahz grumbled. "If I had my way, we'd . . ."

He broke off suddenly and cocked his head to one side.

"You'd better disguise that dragon, kid," he announced suddenly. "And get ready to do your 'dubious character' bit. We're about to have a visitor."

I didn't contest the information. We had established long ago that Aahz's hearing was much more acute than mine.

"Right, Aahz," I acknowledged and hurried about my task.

The trouble with using an inn for a base of operations, however abandoned or weather-beaten it might be, was that occasionally people would stop here seeking food and lodging. Magik was still outlawed in these lands, and the last thing we wanted was witnesses.

Chapter Two:

"First impressions, being the longest lasting, are of utmost importance."
—J. CARTER

AAHZ and I had acquired the inn under rather dubious circumstances. Specifically, we claimed it as our rightful spoils of war after the two of us (with the assistance of a couple of allies, now absent) had routed Isstvan, a maniac magician, and sent him packing into far dimensions along with all his surviving accomplices. The inn had been Isstvan's base of operations. But now it was ours. Who Isstvan had gotten it from and how, I didn't want to know. Despite Aahz's constant assurances, I lived in dread of encountering the inn's rightful owner.

I couldn't help remembering all this as I waited outside the inn for our visitor. As I said, Aahz has very good hearing. When he tells me he hears something "close by," he frequently forgets to mention that "close by" may be over a mile away.

I have also noted, over the course of our friendship, that his hearing is curiously erratic. He can hear

8

a lizard-bird scratching itself half a mile away, but occasionally seems unable to hear the politest of requests no matter how loudly I shout them at him.

There was still no sign of our rumored visitor. I considered moving back inside the inn out of the late morning sun, but decided against it. I had carefully arranged the scene for our guest's arrival, and I hated to disrupt it for such a minor thing as personal comfort.

I had used the disguise spell liberally on Buttercup, Gleep, and myself. Gleep now looked like a unicorn, a change that did not seem to bother Buttercup in the slightest. Apparently unicorns are less discriminating about their playmates than are dragons. I had made them both considerably more disheveled and unkempt-looking than they actually were. This was necessary to maintain the image set forth by my own appearance.

Aahz and I had decided early in our stay that the best way to handle unwanted guests was not to threaten them or frighten them away, but rather to be so repulsive that they left of their own accord. To this end, I had slowly devised a disguise designed to convince strangers they did not want to be in the same inn with me, no matter how large the inn was or how many other people were there. In this disguise, I would greet wayward travelers as the proprietor of the inn.

Modestly, I will admit the disguise was a screaming success. In fact, that was the specific reaction many visitors had to it. Some screamed, some looked ill, others sketched various religious symbols in the air between themselves and me. None of them elected to spend the night.

When I experimented with various physical defects, Aahz correctly pointed out that many people did not find any single defect revolting. In fact, in a dimension such as Klah, most would consider it normal. To guarantee the desired effect, I adopted many of them.

When disguised, I walked with a painful limp, had a hump-back, and a deformed hand which was noticeably diseased. What teeth remained were twisted and stained, and the focus of one of my eyes had a tendency to wander about independently of the other. My nose—in fact, my entire face—was not symmetrical, and as a masterstroke of my disguise abilities, there appeared to be vicious-looking bugs crawling about my mangy hair and tattered clothes.

The overall effect was horrifying. Even Aahz admitted he found it disquieting, which, considering the things he's seen in his travels through the dimensions, was high praise indeed.

My thoughts were interrupted as our visitor came into view. He sat ramrod-straight astride a huge, flightless riding bird. He carried no visible weapons and wore no uniform, but his bearing marked him as a soldier much more than any outer trappings could have. His eyes were wary, constantly darting suspiciously about as he walked his bird up to the inn in slow, deliberate steps. Surprisingly enough, his gaze passed over me several times without registering my presence. Perhaps he didn't realize I was alive.

I didn't like this. The man seemed more the hunter than the casual traveler. Still, he was here and had to be dealt with. I went into my act.

"Does the noble sahr require a room?"

As I spoke I moved forward in my practical, rolling gait. In case the subtlety of my disguise escaped him, I allowed a large gob of spittle to ooze from the corner of my mouth where it rolled unhindered down to my chin.

For a moment the man's attention was occupied controlling his mount. Flightless or not, the bird was trying to take to the air.

Apparently my disguise had touched a primal chord in the bird's mind that went back prior to its flightless ancestry.

I waited, head cocked curiously, while the man fought the bird to a fidgety standstill. Finally, he turned his attention to me for a moment. Then he averted his eyes and stared carefully at the sky.

"I come seeking the one known as Skeeve the magician," he told me.

Now it was my turn to jump. To the best of my knowledge, no one knew who I was and what I was, much less where I was, except for Aahz and me.

"That's me!" I blurted out, forgetting myself and using my real voice.

The man turned horrified eyes on me, and I remembered my appearance.

"That's me master!" I amended hastily. "You wait . . . I fetch."

I turned and scuttled hastily into the inn. Aahz was waiting inside.

"What is it?" he demanded.

"He's . . . he wants to talk to Skeeve . . . to me!" I babbled nervously.

"So?" he asked pointedly. "What are you doing in here? Go outside and talk to the man."

"Looking like this?"

Aahz rolled his eyes at the ceiling in exasperation.

"Who cares what you look like?" he barked. "C'mon, kid. The man's a total stranger!"

"I care!" I declared, drawing myself up haughtily.

"The man asked for Skeeve the magician, and I think—"

"He what?" Aahz interrupted.

"He asked for Skeeve the magician," I repeated, covertly studying the figure waiting outside.

"He looks like a soldier to me," I supplied.

"He looks scared to me," Aahz retorted. "Maybe you should tone down your disguise a bit next time."

"Do you think he's a demon-hunter?" I asked nervously.

Instead of answering my question, Aahz turned abruptly from the window.

"If he wants a magician, we'll give him a magician," he murmured. "Quick, kid, slap the Garkin disguise on me."

As I noted earlier, Garkin was my first magik instructor. An imposing figure with a salt-and-pepper beard, he was one of our favorite and most oft-used disguises. I could do Garkin in my sleep.

"Good enough, kid," Aahz commented, surveying the results of my work. "Now follow close and let me do the talking."

"Like this?" I exclaimed.

"Relax, kid," he reassured me. "For this conversation I'm you. Understand?"

Aahz was already heading out through the door without waiting for my reply, leaving me little choice other than to follow along behind him.

"Who seeks an audience with the great Skeeve?" Aahz bellowed in a resonant bass voice.

The man shot another nervous glance at me, then drew himself up in stiff formality.

"I come as an emissary from his most noble Majesty, Rodrick the Fifth, King of Possiltum, who—"

"Where's Possiltum?" Aahz interrupted.

"I beg your pardon?" the man blinked.

"Possiltum," Aahz repeated. "Where is it?"

"Oh!" the man said with sudden understanding. "It's the kingdom just east of here . . . other side of the Ember River . . . you can't miss it."

"Okay," Aahz nodded. "Go on."

The man took a deep breath, then hesitated, frowning.

"King of Possiltum," I prompted.

"Oh yes! Thanks." The man shot a quick smile, then another quick stare, then continued, "King of Possiltum, who sends his respects and greetings to the one known as Skeeve the magician . . ."

He paused and looked at Aahz expectantly. He was rewarded with a polite nod of the head. Satisfied, the man continued.

"His Majesty extends an invitation to Skeeve the magician to appear before the court of Possiltum that he might be reviewed for his suitability for the position of court magician."

"I don't really feel qualified to pass judgment on the king's suitability as a court magician," Aahz said modestly, eyeing the man carefully. "Isn't he content just to be king?"

"No, no!" the man corrected hastily. "The king wants to review *your* suitability."

"Oh!" Aahz said with the appearance of sudden understanding. "That's a different matter entirely. Well, well. An invitation from . . . who was it again?"

"Rodrick the Fifth," the man announced, lifting his head haughtily.

"Well," Aahz said, grinning broadly. "I've never been one to refuse a *fifth!*"

The man blinked and frowned, then glanced at me quizzically. I shrugged, not understanding the joke myself.

"You may tell His Majesty," Aahz continued, unaware of our confusion. "I shall be happy to accept his kind invitation. I shall arrive at his court at my earliest convenience."

The man frowned.

"I believe His Majesty requires your immediate presence," he commented darkly.

"Of course," Aahz answered smoothly. "How silly of me. If you will accept our hospitality for the night, I and my assistant here will be most pleased to accompany you in the morning."

I knew a cue when I heard one. I drooled and bared my teeth at the messenger.

The man shot a horrified look in my direction.

"Actually," he said hastily, "I really must be going. I'll tell His Majesty you'll be following close behind."

"You're sure you wouldn't like to stay?" Aahz asked hopefully.

"Positive!" The man nearly shouted his reply as he began backing the bird away from us.

"Oh, well," Aahz said. "Perhaps we'll catch up with you on the road."

"In that case," the man said, turning his bird, "I'll want a head . . . that is, I'd best be on my way to announce your coming."

I raised my hand to wave good-bye, but he was already moving at a rapid pace, urging his mount to still greater speeds and ignoring me completely.

"Excellent!" Aahz exclaimed, rubbing his hands together gleefully. "A court magician! What a soft job! And the day started out so miserably."

"If I can interrupt," I interrupted. "There's one minor flaw in your plan."

"Hmm? What's that?"

"I don't want to be a court magician!"

As usual, my protest didn't dampen his enthusiasm at all.

"You didn't want to be a magician, either," he reminded me bluntly. "You wanted to be a thief. Well, here's a good compromise for you. As a court magician, you'll be a civil servant . . . and civil servants are thieves on a grander scale than you ever dreamed possible!"

Chapter Three:

*"Ninety percent of any business trans-
action is selling yourself to the client."*
— X. HOLLANDER

"Now let me see if I've got this right," I said carefully. "You're saying they probably *won't* hire me on
the basis of my abilities?"

I couldn't believe I'd interpreted Aahz's lecture
correctly, but he beamed enthusiastically.

"That's right, kid," he approved. "Now you've
got it."

"No, I don't," I insisted. "That's the craziest
thing I've ever heard!"

Aahz groaned and hid his face in his hand.

It had been like this ever since we left the inn, and
three days of a demon's groaning is a bit much for
anyone to take.

"I'm sorry, Aahz," I said testily, "but I don't
believe it. I've taken a lot of things you've told me on
faith, but this . . . this goes against common sense."

"What does common sense have to do with it?" he
exploded. "We're talking about a job interview!"

At this outburst, Buttercup snorted and tossed his head, making it necessary for us to duck out of range of his horn.

"Steady, Buttercup!" I admonished soothingly.

Though he still rolled his eyes, the unicorn resumed his stoic plodding, the travois loaded with our equipment dragging along behind him still intact. Despite incidents such as had occurred back at the inn, Buttercup and I got along fairly well, and he usually obeyed me. In contrast, he and Aahz never really hit it off, especially when the latter chose to raise his voice angrily.

"All it takes is a little gentleness," I informed Aahz smugly. "You should try it sometime."

"While you're showing off your dubious rapport with animals," Aahz retorted, "you might call your dragon back. All we need is to have him stirring up the countryside."

I cast a quick glance about. He was right. Gleep had disappeared . . . again.

"Gleep!" I called. "Come here, fella!"

"Gleep!" came an answering cry.

The bushes off to our left parted, and the dragon's head emerged.

"Gleep?" he said, cocking his head.

"Come here!" I repeated.

My pet needed no more encouragement. He bounded into the open and trotted to my side.

"I still say we should have left that stupid dragon back at the inn," Aahz grumbled.

I ignored him, checking to be sure that the gear hung saddlebag fashion over the dragon's back was still secure. Personally, I felt we were carrying far too much in the way of personal belongings, but Aahz had insisted. Gleep tried to nuzzle me affectionately with his head, and I caught a whiff of his breath. For a moment, I wondered if Aahz had been right about leaving the dragon behind.

"What were you saying about job interviews?" I asked, both to change the subject and to hide the fact I was gagging.

"I know it sounds ridiculous, kid," Aahz began with sudden sincerity, "and it is, but a lot of things are ridiculous, particularly in this dimension. That doesn't mean we don't have to deal with them."

That gave me pause to think. To a lot of people, having a demon and a dragon for traveling companions would seem ridiculous. As a matter of fact, if I took time to think it through, it seemed pretty ridiculous to me!

"Okay, Aahz," I said finally, "I can accept the existence of ridiculousness as reality. Now try explaining the court magician thing to me again."

We resumed walking as Aahz organized his thoughts. For a change, Gleep trailed placidly along beside Buttercup instead of taking off on another of his exploratory side trips.

"See if this makes any sense," Aahz said finally. "Court magicians don't do much . . . magically at least. They're primarily kept around for show, as a status symbol to demonstrate a court is advanced enough to rate a magician. It's a rare occasion when they're called upon to do anything. If you were a jester, they'd work your tail off, but not as a magician. Remember, most people are skittish about magik, and use it as seldom as possible."

"If that's the case," I said confidently, "I'm qualified. I'll match my ability to do nothing against any magician on Klah."

"No argument there," Aahz observed dryly. "But

it's not quite that easy. To hold the job takes next to no effort at all. Getting the job can be an uphill struggle.''

"Oh!" I said, mollified.

"Now to get the job, you'll have to impress the king and probably his advisors," Aahz continued. "You'll have to impress them with *you*, not with your abilities."

"How's that again?" I frowned.

"Look, kid. Like I said, a court magician is window dressing, a showpiece. They'll be looking for someone they want to have hanging around their court, someone who is impressive whether or not he ever does anything. You'll have to exude confidence. Most important, you'll have to look like a magician . . . or at least, what they think a magician looks like. If you can dress like a magician, talk like a magician, and act like a magician, maybe no one will notice you don't have the abilities of a magician."

"Thanks, Aahz," I grimaced. "You're really doing wonders towards building my confidence."

"Now don't sulk," Aahz admonished. "You know how to levitate reasonably large objects, you can fly after a fashion, and you've got the disguise spell down pat. You're doing pretty well for a rank novice, but don't kid yourself into believing you're anywhere near full magician's status."

He was right, of course, but I was loath to admit it.

"If I'm such a bumbling incompetent," I said stiffly, "why are we on our way to establish me as a court magician?"

Aahz bared his teeth at me in irritation.

"You aren't listening, kid," he snarled. "Holding the job once you've got it will be a breeze. You can handle that now. The tricky part will be getting you hired. Fortunately, with a few minor modifications and a little coaching, I think we can get you ready for polite society."

"Modifications such as what?" I asked, curious despite myself.

Aahz made a big show of surveying me from head to foot.

"For a start," he said, "there's the way you dress."

"What's wrong with the way I dress?" I countered defensively.

"Nothing at all," he replied innocently. "That is, if you want people to see you as a bumpkin peasant with dung on his boots. Of course, if you want to be a court magician, well, that's another story. No respectable magician would be caught dead in an outfit like that."

"But I am a respectable magician!" I argued.

"Really? Respected by who?"

He had me there, so I lapsed into silence.

"That's specifically the reason I had the foresight to bring along a few items from the inn," Aahz continued, indicating Buttercup's burdens with a grand sweep of his hand.

"And here I thought you were just looting the place," I said dryly.

"Watch your mouth, kid," he warned. "This is all for your benefit."

"Really? You aren't expecting anything at all out of this deal?"

My sarcasm, as usual, was lost on him.

"Oh, I'll be around," he acknowledged. "Don't worry about that. Publicly, I'll be your apprentice."

"My apprentice?"

This job was suddenly sounding much better.

"Publicly!" Aahz repeated hastily. "Privately, you'll continue your lessons as normal. Remember that before you start getting frisky with your 'apprentice.' "

"Of course, Aahz," I assured him. "Now, what was it you were saying about changing the way I dress?"

He shot me a sidelong glance, apparently suspicious of my sudden enthusiasm.

"Not that there's anything wrong with me the way I am," I added with a theatrical scowl.

That seemed to ease his doubts.

"Everything's wrong with the way you dress," he growled. "We're lucky those two Imps left most of their wardrobe behind when we sent 'em packing along with Isstvan."

"Higgens and Brockhurst?"

"Yeah, those two," Aahz grinned evilly at the memory. "I'll say one thing for Imps. They may be inferior to Deveels as merchants, but they *are* snappy dressers."

"I find it hard to believe that all that stuff you bundled along is wardrobe," I observed skeptically.

"Of course it isn't," my mentor moaned. "It's special effects gear."

"Special effects?"

"Don't you remember anything, kid?" Aahz scowled. "I told you all this when we first met. However easy magik is, you can't let it *look* easy. You need a few hand props, a line of patter . . . you know, like Garkin had."

Garkin's hut, where I had first been introduced to magik, had been full of candles, vials of strange powders, dusty books . . . now there was a magician's lair! Of course, I had since discovered most of what he had was unnecessary for the actual working of magik itself.

I was beginning to see what Aahz meant when he said I'd have to learn to put on a show.

"We've got a lot of stuff we can work into your presentation," Aahz continued. "Isstvan left a lot of his junk behind when he left. Oh, and you might find some familiar items when we unload. I think the Imps helped themselves to some of Garkin's equipment and brought it back to the inn with them."

"Really?" I said, genuinely interested. "Did they get Garkin's brazier?"

"Brazier?" My mentor frowned.

"You remember," I prompted. "You used it to drink wine out of when you first arrived."

"That's right! Yeah, I think I saw it in there. Why?"

"No special reason," I replied innocently. "It was always a favorite of mine, that's all."

From watching Garkin back in my early apprentice days, I knew there were secrets to that brazier I was dying to learn. I also knew that, if possible, I wanted to save it as a surprise for Aahz.

"We're going to have to do something about your physical appearance, too," Aahz continued thoughtfully.

"What's—"

"You're too young!" he answered, anticipating my question. "Nobody hires a young magician. They want one who's been around for a while. If we—"

He broke off suddenly and craned his neck to look around.

"Kid," he said carefully, studying the sky. "Your dragon's gone again."

I did a fast scan. He was right.

"Gleep!" I called. "Here, fella!"

The dragon's head appeared from the depths of a bush behind us. There was something slimy with legs dangling from his mouth, but before I could manage an exact identification, my pet swallowed and the whatzit disappeared.

"Gleep!" he said proudly, licking his lips with his long forked tongue.

"Stupid dragon," Aahz muttered darkly.

"He's cheap to feed," I countered, playing on what I knew to be Aahz's tight-fisted nature.

As we waited for the dragon to catch up, I had time to reflect that for once I felt no moral or ethical qualms about taking part in one of Aahz's schemes. If the unsuspecting Rodrick the Fifth was taken in by our charade and hired us, I was confident the king would be getting more than he bargained for.

Chapter Four:

*"If the proper preparations have been
made and the necessary precautions
taken, any staged event is guaranteed
success."*

—ETHELRED THE UNREADY

THE candle lit at the barest flick from my mind.

Delighted, I snuffed it and tried again.

A sidelong glance, a fleeting concentration of my
will, and the smoldering wick burst into flame again.

I snuffed the flame and sat smiling at the familiar
candle.

This was the first real proof I'd had as to how far
my magical powers had developed in the past year. I
knew this candle from my years as Garkin's apprentice. In those days, it was my arch nemesis. Even
focusing all my energies failed to light it then. But
now . . .

I glanced at the wick again, and again it rewarded
me with a burst of flame.

I snuffed it and repeated the exercise, my confidence growing as I realized how easily I could now
do something I once thought impossible.

"Will you knock it off with the candle!"

I jumped at the sound of Aahz's outburst, nearly upsetting the candle and setting the blanket afire.

"I'm sorry, Aahz," I said, hastily snuffing the candle for the last time. "I just—"

"You're here to audition for court magician," he interrupted. "Not for town Christmas tree!"

I considered asking what a Christmas tree was, but decided against it. Aahz seemed uncommonly irritable and nervous, and I was pretty sure, however I chose to phrase my question, that the answer would be both sarcastic and unproductive.

"Stupid candle blinking on and off," Aahz grumbled half to himself. "Attract the attention of every guard in the castle."

"I thought we were trying to attract their attention," I pointed out, but Aahz ignored me, peering at the castle through the early-morning light.

He didn't have to peer far, as we were camped in the middle of the road just short of the castle's main gates.

As I said, I was under the impression our position was specifically chosen to attract attention to ourselves.

We had crept into position in the dead of night, clumsily picking our way through the sleeping buildings clustered about the main gate. Not wishing to show a light, unpacking had been minimal, but even in the dark, I had recognized Garkin's candle.

All of this had to do with something Aahz called a "dramatic entrance." As near as I could tell, all this meant was we couldn't do anything the easy way.

Our appearance was also carefully designed for effect, with the aid of the Imps' abandoned wardrobe and my disguise spells.

Aahz was outfitted in my now traditional "dubious character'' disguise. Gleep was standing placidly beside Buttercup disguised as a unicorn, giving us a matched pair. It was my own appearance, however, which had been the main focus of our attentions.

Both Aahz and I had agreed that the Garkin disguise would be unsuitable for this effort. While my own natural appearance was too young, Garkin's would be too old. Since we could pretty much choose the image we wanted, we decided to field a magician in his mid to late thirties; young without being youthful, experienced without being old, and powerful but still learning.

To achieve this disguise involved a bit more work than normal, as I did not have an image in mind to superimpose over my own. Instead, I closed my eyes and envisioned myself as I appeared normally, then slowly erased the features until I had a blank face to begin on. Then I set to work with Aahz watching carefully and offering suggestions and modifications.

The first thing I changed was my height, adjusting the image until the new figure stood a head and a half taller than my actual diminutive stature. My hair was next and I changed my strawberry-blond thatch to a more sinister black, at the same time darkening my complexion several shades.

The face gave us the most trouble.

"Elongate the chin a little more," Aahz instructed. "Put on a beard . . . not that much, stupid! Just a little goatee! . . . That's better! . . . Now lower the sideburns . . . okay, build up the nose . . . narrow it . . . make the eyebrows bushier . . . no, change 'em back and sink the eyes a little instead . . . for crying out loud change the eye color! Make 'em brown . . . okay, now a couple of frown wrinkles in the middle of the forehead. . . . Good. That should do it.''

I stared at the figure in my mind, burning the image into my memory. It was effective, maybe a bit more sinister than I would have designed if left to my own devices, but Aahz was the expert and I had to trust his judgment. I opened my eyes.

"Terrific, kid!" Aahz beamed. "Now put on that black robe with the gold and red trim the Imps left, and you'll cut a figure fit to grace any court."

"Move along there! You're blocking the road!"

The rude order wrenched my thoughts back to the present.

A soldier, resplendent in leather armor and brandishing an evil-looking pike, was angrily approaching our crude encampment. Behind him the gates stood slightly ajar, and I could see the heads of several other soldiers watching us curiously.

Now that the light was improving, I could see the wall better. It wasn't much of a wall, barely ten feet high. That figured. From what we had seen since we crossed the border, it wasn't much of a kingdom, either.

"You deaf or something?" the soldier barked drawing close. "I said move along!"

Aahz scuttled forward and planted himself in the soldier's path.

"Skeeve the Magnificent has arrived," he announced. "And he—"

"I don't care who you are!" the soldier snarled, wasting no time placing his pike between himself and the figure addressing him. "You can't—"

He broke off abruptly as his pike leaped from his grasp and floated horizontally in mid-air until it was forming a barricade between him and Aahz.

The occurrence was my doing, a simple feat of levitation. Regardless of our planned gambit, I felt I

should take a direct hand in the proceedings before
things got completely out of hand.

"I am Skeeve!" I boomed, forcing my voice into a
resonant bass. "And that is my assistant you are at-
tempting to threaten with your feeble weapon. We
have come in response to an invitation from Rodrick
the Fifth, King of Possiltum!"

"That's right, Bosco!" Aahz leered at the soldier.
"Now just run along like a good fellow and pass the
word we're here . . . eh?"

As I noted earlier, all this was designed to impress
the hell out of the general populace. Apparently the
guard hadn't read the script. He did not cower in
terror or cringe with fear. If anything, our little act
seemed to have the exact opposite effect on him.

"A magician, eh?" he said with a mocking sneer.
"For that I've got standing orders. Go around to the
back where the others are."

This took us aback. Well, at least it took *me*
aback. According to our plan, we would end up argu-
ing whether we entered the palace to perform in the
king's court, or if the king had to bring his court outside to where we were. Being sent to the back door
was not an option we had considered.

"To the back?" Aahz glowered. "You dare to suggest a magician of my master's stature go to the back
door like a common servant?"

The soldier didn't budge an inch.

"If it were up to me, I'd 'dare to suggest' a far less
pleasant activity for you. As it is, I have my orders.
You're to go around to the back like all the others."

"Others?" I asked carefully.

"That's right," the guard sneered. "The king is
holding an open air court to deal with all you
'miracle workers.' Every hack charm-peddler for

eight kingdoms is in town. Some of 'em have been in line since noon yesterday. Now get around to the back and quit blocking the road!''

With that he turned on his heel and marched back to the gate, leaving his pike hanging in mid-air.

For once, Aahz was as speechless as I was. Apparently I wasn't the only one the king had invited to drop by. Apparently we were in big trouble.

Chapter Five:

". . . Eye of newt, toe of frog . . . "
—Believed to be the first recipe
for an explosive mixture . . .
The forerunner of gunpowder.

"WHAT are we going to do, Aahz?"

With the guard out of earshot, I could revert to my normal voice and speech patterns, though it was still necessary to keep my physical disguise intact.

"That's easy," he responded. "We pack up our things and go around the back. Weren't you listening, kid?"

"But what are we going to do about . . ."

But Aahz was already at work, rebinding the few items we had unpacked.

"Don't do anything, kid," he warned over his shoulder. "We can't let anyone see you doing menial work. It's bad for the image."

"He said there were other magicians here!" I blurted at last.

"Yeah. So?"

"Well, what are we going to do?"

Aahz scowled. "I told you once. We're going to pack our things and—"

"What are we going to do about the other magicians?"

"Do? We aren't going to *do* anything. You aren't up to dueling, you know."

He had finished packing and stepped back to survey his handiwork. Nodding in satisfaction, he turned and shot a glance over my shoulder.

"Do something about the pike, will ya, kid?"

I followed his gaze. The guard's pike was still hanging suspended in mid-air. Even though I hadn't been thinking about it, part of my mind had been keeping it afloat until I decided what to do with it. The question was, what should I do with it?

"Say, Aahz . . ." I began, but Aahz had already started walking along the wall.

For a moment I was immobilized with indecision. The guard had gone so I couldn't return his weapon to him. Still, simply letting it drop to the ground seemed somehow anticlimatic.

Unable to think of anything to do that would have the proper dramatic flair, I decided to postpone the decision. For the time being, I let the pike float along behind me as I hurried after Aahz, first giving it additional elevation so it would not be a danger to Gleep and Buttercup.

"Were you expecting other magicians to be here?" I asked, drawing abreast of my mentor.

"Not really," Aahz admitted. "It was a possibility, of course, but I didn't give it a very high probability rating. Still, it's not all that surprising. A job like this is bound to draw competition out of the woodwork."

He didn't seem particularly upset, so I tried to take

this new development in stride.

"Okay," I said calmly. "How does this change our plans?"

"It doesn't. Just do your thing like I showed you and everything should come out fine."

"But if the other magicians—"

Aahz stopped short and turned to face me.

"Look, kid," he said seriously, "just because I keep telling you you've got a long way to go before you're a master magician doesn't mean you're a hack! I wouldn't have encouraged you to show up for this interview if I didn't think you were good enough to land the job."

"Really, Aahz?"

He turned and started walking again.

"Just remember, as dimensions go, Klah isn't noted for its magicians. You're no master, but masters are few and far between. I'm betting that compared to the competition, you'll look like a real expert."

That made sense. Aahz was quite outspoken in his low opinion of Klah and the Klahds that inhabited it, including me. That last thought made me fish for a bit more reassurance.

"Aahz?"

"Yeah, kid?"

"What's your honest appraisal of my chances?"

There was a moment of silence before he answered.

"Kid, you know how you're always complaining that I keep tearing down your confidence?"

"Yeah?"

"Well, for both our sakes, don't push too hard for my honest appraisal."

I didn't.

Getting through the back gate proved to be no problem . . . mostly because there wasn't a back gate. To my surprise and Aahz's disgust, the wall did not extend completely around the palace. As near as I could see, only the front wall was complete. The two side walls were under construction, and the back wall was nonexistent. I should clarify that. My statement that the side walls were under construction was an assumption based on the presence of scaffolding at the end of the wall rather than by the observation of any activity going on. If there was any work being performed, it was being done carefully enough not to disturb the weeds which abounded throughout the scaffolding.

I was beginning to have grave doubts about the kingdom I was about to ally myself with.

It was difficult to tell if the court was being convened in a garden, or if this was a courtyard losing its fight with the weeds and underbrush which crowded in through the opening where the back wall should have been. (Having grown up on a farm, my basic education in plants was that if it wasn't edible and growing in neat rows, it was a weed.)

As if in answer to my thoughts, Buttercup took a large mouthful of the nearest clump of growth and began chewing enthusiastically. Gleep sniffed the same bush and turned up his nose at it.

All this I noted only as an aside. My main attention was focused on the court itself.

There was a small open-sided pavilion set against the wall of the palace sheltering a seated figure, presumably the king. Standing close beside him on either side were two other men. The crowd, such as it was, was split into two groups. The first was standing in a somewhat orderly line along one side of the garden. I

assumed this was the waiting line . . . or rather I
hoped it was as that was the group we joined. The
second group was standing in a disorganized mob on
the far side of the garden watching the proceedings.
Whether these were rejected applicants or merely interested hangers-on, I didn't know.

Suddenly, a young couple in the watching group
caught my eye. I hadn't expected to encounter any
familiar faces here, but these two I had seen before.
Not only had I seen them, Aahz and I had imperson-
ated them at one point, a charade which had resulted
in our being hanged.

"Aahz!" I whispered urgently. "Do you see those
two over there?"

"No," Aahz said bluntly, not even turning his
head to look.

"But they're the—"

"Forget 'em," he insisted. "Watch the judges.
They're the ones we have to impress."

I had to admit that made a certain amount of
sense. Grudgingly, I turned my attention to the
figures in the pavilion.

The king was surprisingly young, perhaps in his
mid-twenties. His hair was a tumble of shoulder-
length curls, which combined with his slight build
almost made him look effeminate. Judging from his
posture, either the interviews had been going on for
some time, or he had mastered the art of looking
totally bored.

The man on his left bent and urgently whispered
something in the king's ear and was answered by a
vague nod.

This man, only slightly older than the king but
balding noticeably, was dressed in a tunic and cloak

of drab color and conservative cut. Though relaxed in posture and quiet in bearing, there was a watchful brightness to his eyes that reminded me of a feverish weasel.

There was a stirring of the figure on the king's right, which drew my attention in that direction. I had a flash impression of a massive furry lump, then I realized with a start that it was a man. He was tall and broad, his head crowned with thick, black, unkempt curls, his face nearly obscured by a full beard and mustache. This, combined with his heavy fur cloak, gave him an animal-like appearance which had dominated my first impression. He spoke briefly to the king, then recrossed his arms in a gesture of finality and glared at the other advisor. His cloak opened briefly during his oration, giving me a glimpse of a glittering shirt of mail and a massive double-headed hand-axe hung on a belt at his waist. Clearly this was not a man to cross. The balding figure seemed unimpressed, matching his rival's glare with one of his own.

There was a sharp nudge in my ribs.

"Did you see that?" Aahz whispered urgently.

"See what?" I asked.

"The king's advisors. A general and a chancellor unless I miss my guess. Did you see the gold medallion on the general?"

"I saw his axe!" I whispered back.

The light in the courtyard suddenly dimmed.

Looking up, I saw a mass of clouds forming overhead, blotting out the sun.

"Weather control," Aahz murmured half to himself. "Not bad."

Sure enough, the old man in the red cloak currently before the throne gestured wildly and tossed a cloud of purple powder into the air, and a light drizzle began to fall.

My spirits fell along with the rain. Even with Aahz's coaching on presentation, my magik was not this powerful or impressive.

"Aahz . . ." I whispered urgently.

Instead of responding, he waved me to silence, his eyes riveted on the pavilion.

Following his gaze, I saw the general speaking urgently with the king. The king listened for a moment, then shrugged and said something to the magician.

Whatever he said, the magician didn't like it. Drawing himself up haughtily, he turned to leave, only to be called back by the king. Pointing to the clouds, the king said a few more words and leaned back. The magician hesitated, then shrugged, and began gesturing and chanting once more.

"Turned him down," Aahz said smugly.

"Then what's he doing now?"

"Clearing up the rain before the next act goes on," Aahz informed me.

Sure enough, the drizzle was slowing and the clouds began to scatter, much to the relief of the audience who, unlike the king, had no pavilion to protect them from the storm. This further display of the magician's power, however, did little to bolster my sagging confidence.

"Aahz!" I whispered. "He's a better magician than I am."

"Yeah," Aahz responded. "So?"

"So if they turned him down, I haven't got a chance!"

"Maybe yes, maybe no," came the thoughtful

reply. "As near as I can tell, they're looking for something specific. Who knows? Maybe you're it. Remember what I told you, cushy jobs don't always go to the most skillful. In fact, it usually goes the other way."

"Yeah," I said, trying to sound optimistic. "Maybe I'll get lucky."

"It's going to take more than luck," Aahz corrected me sternly. "Now, what have you learned watching the king's advisors?"

"They don't like each other," I observed immediately.

"Right!" Aahz sounded surprised and pleased. "Now that means you probably won't be able to please them both. You'll have to play up to one of them . . . or better still insult one. That'll get the other one on your side faster than anything. Now, which one do you want on your side?"

That was easier than his first question.

"The general," I said firmly.

"Wrong! You want the chancellor."

"The chancellor!" I exclaimed, blurting the words out louder than I had intended. "Did you see the size of that axe the general's carrying?"

"Uh-huh," Aahz replied. "Did you hear what happened to the guy who interviewed before old Red Cloak here got his turn?"

I closed my eyes and controlled my first sharp remark.

"Aahz," I said carefully, "remember me? I'm Skeeve. I'm the one who can't hear whispers a mile away."

As usual Aahz ignored my sarcasm.

"The last guy didn't even get a chance to show his stuff," he informed me. "The chancellor took one look at the crowd he brought with him and asked how many were in his retinue. 'Eight,' the man said. 'Too many!' says the chancellor and the poor fool was dismissed immediately.''

"So?" I asked bluntly.

"So the chancellor is the one watching the purse strings,'' concluded Aahz. "What's more, he has more influence than the general. Look at these silly walls. Do you think a military man would leave walls half-finished if he had the final say? Somebody decided too much money was being spent constructing them and the project was canceled or delayed. I'm betting that somebody was the chancellor."

"Maybe they ran out of stones," I suggested.

"C'mon, kid. From what we've seen since we crossed the border this kingdom's principal crop is stones.''

"But the general . . ."

As I spoke, I glanced in the general's direction again. To my surprise and discomfort, he was staring directly at me. It wasn't a friendly stare.

I hesitated for a moment, hoping I was wrong. I wasn't. The general's gaze didn't waver, nor did his expression soften. If anything, it got uglier.

"Aahz," I hissed desperately, unable to tear my eyes from the general.

Now the king and the chancellor were staring in my direction too, their attention drawn by the general's gaze.

"Kid!" Aahz moaned beside me. "I thought I told you to do something about that pike!"

The pike! I had completely forgotten about it!

I pulled my eyes from the general's glare and glanced behind me as casually as I could.

Buttercup and Gleep were still standing patiently

to our rear, and floating serenely above them was the guard's pike. I guess it was kind of noticeable.

"You!"

I turned toward the pavilion and the sound of the bellow. The general had stepped forward and was pointing a massive finger at me.

"Yes, you!" he roared as our eyes met once more. "Where did you get that pike? It belongs to the palace guards."

"I think you're about to have your interview, kid," Aahz murmured. "Give it your best and knock 'em stiff."

"But—" I protested.

"It beats standing in line!"

With that, Aahz took a long leisurely step backward. The effect was the same as if I had stepped forward, which I definitely hadn't. With the attention of the entire courtyard now centered on me, however, I had no choice but to take the plunge.

Chapter Six:

"That's entertainment!"

—VLAD THE IMPALER

CROSSING my arms, I moved toward the pavilion, keeping my pace slow and measured.

Aahz had insisted I practice this walk. He said it would make me look confident and self-possessed. Now that I was actually appearing before a king, I found I was using the walk, not as a show of arrogance, but to hide the weakness in my legs.

"Well?" the general rumbled, looming before me. "I asked you a question! Where did you get that pike? You'd best answer before I grow angry!"

Something in me snapped. Any fear I felt of the general and his axe evaporated, replaced by a heady glow of strength.

I had discovered on my first visit to the Bazaar at Deva that I didn't like to be pushed by big, loud Deveels. I discovered now that I also didn't like it any better when the arrogance came from a big, loud fellow Klahd.

So the big man wanted to throw his weight around, did he?

With a twitch of my mind, I summoned the pike. Without turning to look, I brought it arrowing over my shoulder in a course destined to embed it in the general's chest.

The general saw it coming and paled. He took an awkward step backward, realized it was too late for flight, and groped madly for his axe.

I stopped the pike three feet from his chest, floating it in front of him with its point leveled at his heart.

"This pike?" I asked casually.

"Ahh . . ." the general responded, his eyes never leaving the weapon.

"I took this pike from an overly rude soldier. He said he was following orders. Would those orders come from you, by any chance?"

"I . . . um. . . ." The general licked his lips. "I issued orders that my men deal with strangers in an expedient fashion. I said nothing about their being less then polite."

"In that case . . ."

I moved the pike ninety degrees so that it no longer threatened the general.

". . . I return the pike to you so that you might give it back to the guard along with a clarification of your orders. . . ."

The general hesitated, scowling, then extended his hand to grasp the floating pike. Just before he reached it, I let it fall to the ground where it clattered noisily.

". . . and hopefully additional instructions as to how to handle their weapons," I concluded.

The general flushed and started to pick up the

pike. Then the chancellor snickered, and the general spun around to glare at him. The chancellor smirked openly and whispered something to the king, who tried to suppress a smile at his words.

The general turned to me again, ignoring the pike, and glared down from his full height.

"Who are you?" he asked in a tone which implied my name would be immediately moved to the head of the list for public execution.

"Who's asking?" I glared back, still not completely over my anger.

"The man you are addressing," the king interceded, "is Hugh Badaxe, Commander of the Royal Armies of Possiltum."

"And I am J. R. Grimble," the chancellor added hastily, afraid of being left out. "First Advisor to His Majesty."

The general shot another black look at Grimble. I decided it was time to get down to business.

"I am the magician known as Skeeve," I began grandly. "I have come in response to a gracious invitation from His Most Noble Majesty, Rodrick the Fifth."

I paused and inclined my head slightly to the king who smiled and nodded in return.

"I have come to determine for myself if I should consider accepting a position at the court of Possiltum."

The phrasing of that last part had been chosen very carefully by Aahz. It was designed to display my confidence by implying the choice was mine rather than theirs.

The subtlety was not lost on the chancellor, who raised a critical eyebrow at my choice of words.

"Now, such a position requires confidence on both

sides," I continued. "I must feel that I will be amply rewarded for my services, and His Majesty must be satisfied that my skills are worthy of his sponsorship."

I turned slightly and raised my voice to address the entire court.

"The generosity of the crown of Possiltum is known to all," I declared. "And I have every confidence His Majesty will reward his retainers in proportion to their service to him."

There was a strangled sound behind me, from the general, I think. I ignored it.

"Therefore, all that is required is that I satisfy His Majesty . . . and his advisors . . . that my humble skills will indeed suffice his needs."

I turned to the throne once more, letting the king see my secret smile which belied the humility of my words.

"Your Majesty, my powers are many and varied. However, the essence of power is control. Therefore realizing you are a busy man, rather than waste time with mere commercial trickeries and minor demonstrations such as we have already seen, I shall weave but three spells and trust in your wisdom to perceive the depths behind them."

I turned and stretched forth a finger to point at Buttercup and Gleep.

"Yonder are my prize pair of matched unicorns," I said dramatically. "Would Your Majesty be so kind as to choose one of them?"

The king blinked in surprise at being invited to participate in my demonstration. For a moment he hesitated.

"Umm . . . I choose the one on the left," he said, finally indicating Buttercup.

I bowed slightly.

"Very well, Your Majesty. By your word shall that creature be spared. Observe the other closely."

Actually, that was another little stunt Aahz had taught me. It's called a "magician's force," and allows a performer to offer his audience a choice without really giving them a choice. Had the king chosen Gleep, I would have simply proceeded to work on "the creature he had doomed with a word."

Slowly, I pointed a finger at Gleep and lowered my head slightly.

"*Walla walla Washington!*" I said somberly.

I don't know what the words meant, but Aahz assured me they had historic precedence and would convince people I was actually doing something complex.

"*Alla kazam shazam,*" I continued, raising my other arm. "*Bibbity bobbity . . .*"

I mentally removed Gleep's disguise.

The crowd reacted with a gasp, drowning out my final "*goo-gleep.*"

My dragon heard his name, though, and reacted immediately. His head came up and he lumbered forward to stand docilely at my side. As planned, Aahz immediately shambled forward to a position near Gleep's head and stood watchful and ready.

This was meant to imply that we were prepared to handle any difficulty which might arise with the dragon. The crowd's reaction to him, however, overshadowed their horror at seeing a unicorn transformed to a dragon. I had forgotten how effective the "disreputable character" disguise was. Afraid of losing the momentum of my performance, I hurried on.

"This misshapen wretch is my apprentice Aahz," I

announced. "You may wonder if it is within his power to stop the dragon should the beast grow angry. I tell you now . . . it is not!"

The crowd edged back nervously. From the corner of my eye, I saw the general's hand slide to the handle of his axe.

"But it *is* within my power! Now you know that the forces of darkness are no strangers to Skeeve!"

I spun and stabbed a finger at Aahz.

"*Bobbelty gook, crumbs and martyrs!*"

I removed Aahz's disguise.

There was a moment of stunned silence, then Aahz smiled. Aahz's smile has been known to make strong men weak, and there were not many strong men in the crowd.

The audience half trampled each other in their haste to backpedal from the demon, and the sound of screeches was intermixed with hastily chanted protection spells.

I turned to the throne once more. The king and the chancellor seemed to be taking it well. They were composed, though a bit pale. The general was scowling thoughtfully at Aahz.

"As a demon, my apprentice can suppress the dragon if need be . . . nay, ten dragons. Such is my power. Yet power must be tempered with gentleness . . . gentility if you will."

I allowed my expression to grow thoughtful.

"To confuse one's enemies and receive one's allies, you need no open show of power or menace. For occasions such as those, one's powers can be masked until one is no more conspicuous than . . . than a stripling."

As I spoke the final words, I stripped away my own disguise and stood in my youthful unsplendor. I

probably should have used some fake magik words,
but I had already used up all the ones Aahz had
taught me and was afraid of experimenting with new
ones.

The king and the chancellor were staring at me in-
tently as if trying to penetrate my magical disguise
with willpower alone. The general was performing a
similar exercise staring at Aahz, who folded his arms
and bared his teeth in a confident smile.

For a change, I shared his confidence. Let them
stare. It was too late to penetrate my magik because I
wasn't working any more. Though the royal troupe
and the entire audience was convinced they were wit-
nessing a powerful spell, in actuality all I had done
was remove the spells which had been distorting their
vision. At the moment, all of us, Aahz, Buttercup,
Gleep, and myself, were our normal selves, however
abnormal we appeared. Even the most adept magical
vision could not penetrate a nonexistent spell.

"As you see, Your Majesty," I concluded. "My
powers are far from ordinary. They can make the
gentle fearsome, or the mighty harmless. They can
destroy your enemies or amuse your court, depending upon your whim. Say the word, speak your
approval, and the powers of Skeeve are yours to
command."

I drew myself up and bowed my head respectfully,
and remained in that position awaiting judgment
from the throne.

Several moments passed without a word. Finally, I
risked a peek at the pavilion.

The chancellor and the general were exchanging
heated whispers over the head of the king, who inclined his head this way and that as he listened.
Realizing this could take a while, I quietly eased my

head to an upright position as I waited.

"Skeeve!" the king called suddenly, interrupting his advisor's arguments. "That thing you did with the pike. Can you always control weapons so easily?"

"Child's play, Your Majesty," I said modestly. "I hesitate to even acknowledge it as a power."

The king nodded and spoke briefly to his advisors in undertones. When he had finished, the general flushed and, turning on his heel, strode off into the palace. The chancellor looked smug.

I risked a glance at Aahz, who winked at me. Even though he was further away, apparently his acute hearing had given him advance notice of the king's decision.

"Let all here assembled bear witness!" the chancellor's ringing voice announced. "Rodrick the Fifth, King of Possiltum, does hereby commend the magical skill and knowledge of one Skeeve and does formally name him Magician to the Court of Possiltum. Let all applaud the appointment of this master magician . . . and then disperse!"

There was a smattering of halfhearted applause from my vanquished rivals, and more than a few glares. I acknowledged neither as I tried to comprehend the chancellor's words.

I did it! Court Magician! Of the entire selection of magicians from five kingdoms, I had been chosen! Me! Skeeve!

I was suddenly aware of the chancellor beckoning me forward. Trying to be nonchalant, I approached the throne.

"Lord Magician," the chancellor said with a smile. "If you will, might we discuss the matter of your wages?"

"My apprentice handles such matters," I informed him loftily. "I prefer not to distract myself with such mundane matters."

Again, we had agreed that Aahz would handle the wage negotiations, his knowledge of magik being surpassed only by his skill at haggling. I turned and beckoned to him. He responded by hurrying forward, his eavesdropping having forewarned him of the situation.

"That can wait, Grimble," the king interrupted. "There are more pressing matters which command our magician's attention."

"You need only command, Your Majesty," I said, bowing grandly.

"Fine," the king beamed. "Then report to General Badaxe immediately for your briefing."

"Briefing about what?" I asked, genuinely puzzled.

"Why, your briefing about the invading army, of course," the king replied.

An alarm gong went off in the back of my mind.

"Invading army?" I blurted, forgetting my rehearsed pompous tones. "What invading army?"

"The one which even now approaches our borders," the chancellor supplied. "Why else would we suddenly need a magician?"

Chapter Seven:

"Numerical superiority is of no conse-
quence. In battle, victory will go to the
best tactician."

—G. A. CUSTER

"CUSHY job, he said! Chance to practice, he said!
Piece of cake, he said!"

"Simmer down, kid!" Aahz growled.

"Simmer down? Aahz, weren't you listening? I'm
supposed to stop an army! Me!"

"It could be worse," Aahz insisted.

"How?" I asked bluntly.

"You could be doing it without me," he replied.
"Think about it."

I did, and cooled down immediately. Even though
my association with Aahz seemed to land me in an in-
ordinate amount of trouble, he had also been unfail-
ing in his ability to get me out . . . so far. The last
thing I wanted to do was drive him away just when I
needed him the most.

"What am I going to do, Aahz?" I moaned.

"Since you ask"—Aahz smiled—"my advice
would be to not panic until we get the whole story.

Remember, there are armies and there are armies. For all we know, this one might be weak enough for us to beat fair and square.''

"And if it isn't?" I asked skeptically.

"We'll burn that bridge when we come to it," Aahz sighed. "First, let's hear what old Badaxe has to say."

Not being able to think of anything to say in reply to that, I didn't. Instead, I kept pace with my mentor in gloomy silence as we followed the chancellor's directions through the corridors of the palace.

It would have been easier to accept the offered guide to lead us to our destination, but I had been more than a little eager to speak with Aahz privately. Consequently, we had left Buttercup and Gleep in the courtyard with our equipment and were seeking out the general's chambers on our own.

The palace was honeycombed with corridors to the point where I wondered if there weren't more corridors than rooms. Our trek was made even more difficult by the light, or lack thereof. Though there were numerous mountings for torches set in the walls, it seemed only about one out of every four was being used, and the light shed by those torches was less than adequate for accurate navigation of the labyrinth.

I commented on this to Aahz as further proof of the tightfisted nature of the kingdom. His curt response was that the more money they saved on overhead and maintenance, the more they would have to splurge on luxuries . . . like us.

He was doggedly trying to explain the concept of an "energy crisis" to me, when we rounded a corner and sighted the general's quarters.

They were fairly easy to distinguish, since this was

the only door we had encountered which was brack-
eted by a pair of matching honor guards. Their polished armor gleamed from broad shoulders as they
observed our approach through narrowed eyes.

"Are these the quarters of General Badaxe?" I inquired politely.

"Are you the magician called Skeeve?" the guard
challenged back.

"The kid asked you a question, soldier!" Aahz interceded. "Now are you going to answer or are you
so dumb you don't know what's on the other side of
the door you're guarding?"

The guard flushed bright red, and I noticed his
partner's knuckles whitening on the pike he was grip-
ping. It occurred to me that now that I had landed
the magician's job, it might not be the wisest course
to continue antagonizing the military.

"Um, Aahz . . ." I murmured.

"Yes! These are the quarters of General Badaxe
. . . sir!" the guard barked suddenly.

Apparently the mention of my colleague's name
had confirmed my identity, though I wondered how
many strangers could be wandering the halls accompanied by large scaly demons. The final, painful,
"sir" was a tribute to my performance in the courtyard. Apparently the guards had been instructed to
be polite, at least to me, no matter how much it hurt
. . . which it obviously did.

"Thank you, guard," I said loftily, and hammered
on the door with my fist.

"Further," the guard observed, "the general left
word that you were to go right in."

The fact that he had withheld that bit of information until after I had knocked indicated that the
guards hadn't completely abandoned their low

regard for magicians. They were simply finding more subtle ways of being annoying.

I realized Aahz was getting ready to start a new round with the guard, so I hastily opened the door and entered, forcing him to follow.

The general was standing at the window, silhouetted by the light streaming in from outside. As we entered, he turned to face us.

"Ah! Come in, gentlemen," he boomed in a mellow tone. "I've been expecting you. Do make yourselves comfortable. Help yourselves to the wine if you wish."

I found his sudden display of friendliness even more disquieting than his earlier show of hostility. Aahz, however, took it all in stride, immediately taking up the indicated jug of wine. For a moment I thought he was going to pour a bit of it into one of the goblets which shared the tray with the jug and pass it to me. Instead, he took a deep drink directly from the jug and kept it, licking his lips in appreciation. In the midst of the chaos my life had suddenly become, it was nice to know some things remained constant.

The general frowned at the display for a moment, then forced his features back into the jovial expression he had first greeted us with.

"Before we begin the briefing," he smiled, "I must apologize for my rude behavior during the interview. Grimble and I have . . . differed in our opinions on the existing situation, and I'm afraid I took it out on you. For that I extend my regrets. Ordinarily, I would have nothing against magicians as a group, or you specifically."

"Whoa! Back up a minute, General," Aahz interrupted. "How does your feud with the chancellor involve us?"

The general's eyes glittered with a fierceness that belied the gentility of his oration.

"It's an extension of our old argument concerning allocation of funds," he said. "When news reached us of the approaching force, my advice to the king was to immediately strengthen our own army that we might adequately perform our sworn duty of defending the realm."

"Sounds like good advice to me," I interjected, hoping to improve my status with the general by agreeing with him.

Badaxe responded by fixing me with a hard glare.

"Strange that you should say that, magician," he observed stonily. "Grimble's advice was to invest the money elsewhere than in the army, specifically in a magician."

It suddenly became clear why we had been received by the guards and the general with something less than open-armed camaraderie. Not only were they getting us instead of reinforcements, our presence was a slap at their abilities.

"Okay, General," Aahz acknowledged. "All that's water under the drawbridge. What are we up against?"

The general glanced back and forth between me and Aahz, apparently surprised that I was allowing my apprentice to take the lead in the briefing. When I failed to rebuke Aahz for his forwardness, the general shrugged and moved to a piece of parchment hanging on the wall.

"I believe the situation is shown clearly by this—" he began.

"What's that?" Aahz interrupted.

The general started to respond sharply, then caught himself. "This," he said evenly, "is a map of the kingdom you are supposed to defend. It's called Possiltum."

"Yes, of course," I nodded. "Continue."

"This line here to the north of our border represents the advancing army you are to deal with."

"Too bad you couldn't get it to scale," Aahz commented. "The way you have it there, the enemy's front is longer than your border."

The general bared his teeth.

"The drawing *is* to scale," he said pointedly. "Perhaps now you will realize the magnitude of the task before you."

My mind balked at accepting his statement.

"Really, General," I chided. "Surely you're overstating the case. There aren't enough fighting men in any kingdom to form a front that long."

"Magician," the general's voice was menacing, "I did not reach my current rank by overstating military situations. The army you are facing is one of the mightiest forces the world has ever seen. It is the striking arm of a rapidly growing empire situated far to the north. They have been advancing for three years now, absorbing smaller kingdoms and crushing any resistance offered. All able-bodied men of conquered lands are conscripted for military service, swelling their ranks to the size you see indicated on the map. The only reason they are not advancing faster is that in addition to limitless numbers of men, they possess massive war machines which, though effective, are slow to transport."

"Now tell us the bad news," Aahz commented dryly.

The general took him seriously.

"The bad news," he growled, "is that their leader is a strategist without peer. He rose to power trouncing forces triple the size of his own numbers, and now that he has a massive army at his command, he is virtually unbeatable."

"I'm beginning to see why the king put his money into a magician," my mentor observed. "It doesn't look like you could have assembled a force large enough to stop them."

"That wasn't my plan!" the general bristled. "While we may not have been able to crush the enemy, we could have made them pay dearly enough for crossing our border that they might have turned aside for weaker lands easier to conquer."

"You know, Badaxe," Aahz said thoughtfully, "that's not a bad plan. Working together we might still pull it off. How many men can you give us for support?"

"None," the general said firmly.

I blinked.

"Excuse me, General," I pressed. "For a moment there, I thought you said—"

"None," he repeated. "I will not assign a single soldier of mine to support your campaign."

"That's insane!" Aahz exploded. "How do you expect us to stop an army like that with just magik?"

"I don't," the general smiled.

"But if we fail," I pointed out, "Possiltum falls."

"That is correct," Badaxe replied calmly.

"But—"

"Allow me to clarify my position," he interrupted. "In my estimation, there is more at stake here than one kingdom. If you succeed in your mission, it will establish that magik is more effective than military force in defending a kingdom. Eventually, that could lead to all armies being disbanded in preference to hiring magicians. I will have no part in establishing a precedent such as that. If you want to show that magicians are superior to armies, you will have to do it with magik alone. The military will not lift a finger to assist you."

As he spoke, he took the jug of wine from Aahz's unresisting fingers, a sign in itself that Aahz was as stunned by the general's words as I was.

"My feelings on this subject are very strong, gentlemen," Badaxe continued, pouring himself some wine. "So strong, in fact, I am willing to sacrifice myself and my kingdom to prove the point. What is more, I would strongly suggest that you do the same."

He paused, regarding us with those glittering eyes.

"Because I tell you here and now, should you emerge victorious from the impending battle, you will not live to collect your reward. The king may rule the court, but word of what happens in the kingdom comes to him through my soldiers, and those soldiers will be posted along your return path to the palace, with orders to bring back word of your accidental demise, even if they have to arrange it. Do I make myself clear?"

Chapter Eight:

"Anything worth doing, is worth doing for a profit."

—TERESIAS

WITH a massive effort of self-control, I contained myself not only after we had left the general's quarters, but until we were out of earshot of the honor guard. When I finally spoke, I managed to keep the telltale note of hysteria out of my voice which would have betrayed my true feelings.

"Like you said, Aahz," I commented casually, "there are armies and there are armies. Right?"

Aahz wasn't fooled for a minute.

"Hysterics won't get us anywhere, kid," he observed. "What we need is sound thinking."

"Excuse me," I said pointedly, "but isn't 'sound thinking' what got us into the mess in the first place?"

"Okay, okay!" Aahz grimaced. "I'll admit I made a few oversights when I originally appraised the situation."

"A few oversights?" I echoed incredulously. "Aahz, this 'cushy job' you set me up for doesn't bear even the vaguest resemblance to what you described when you sold me on the idea."

"I know, kid," Aahz sighed. "I definitely owe you an apology. This sounds like it's actually going to be work."

"Work!" I shrieked, losing control slightly. "It's going to be suicide."

Aahz shook his head sadly.

"There you go overreacting again. It doesn't have to be suicide. We've got a choice, you know."

"Sure," I retorted sarcastically. "We can get killed by the invaders or we can get killed by Badaxe's boys. How silly of me not to have realized it. For a moment there I was getting worried."

"Our choice," Aahz corrected sternly, "is to go through with this lame-brained mission, or to take the money and run."

A ray of hope broke through the dismal gloom that had burdened my mind.

"Aahz," I said in genuine awe, "you're a genius. C'mon, let's get going."

"Get going where?" Aahz asked.

"Back to the inn, of course," I replied. "The sooner the better."

"That wasn't one of our options," my mentor sneered.

"But you said—"

"I said 'take the money *and* run' not just 'run,' " he corrected. "We aren't going anywhere until we've seen Grimble."

"But Aahz—"

" 'But Aahz' nothing," he interrupted fiercely. "This little jaunt has cost us a bundle. We're going to at least make it break even, if not show a small profit."

"It hasn't cost us anything," I said bluntly.

"It cost us travel time and time away from your studies," Aahz countered. "That's worth something."

"But—"

"Besides," he continued loftily, "there are more important issues at stake here."

"Like what?" I pressed.

"Well . . . like, um . . ."

"There you are, gentlemen!"

We turned to find Grimble approaching us rapidly from behind.

"I was hoping to catch you after the briefing," the chancellor continued, joining us. "Do you mind if I watch with you? I know you'll be eager to start off on your campaign, but there are certain matters we *must* discuss before you leave."

"Like our wages," Aahz supplied firmly.

Grimble's smile froze.

"Oh! Yes, of course. First, however, there are other things to deal with. I trust the general supplied you with the necessary information for your mission."

"Down to the last gruesome detail," I confirmed.

"Good, good," the chancellor chortled, his enthusiasm undimmed by my sarcasm. "I have every confidence you'll be able to deal with the riffraff from the North. I'll have you know you were my personal choice even before the interviews. In fact, I was the one responsible for sending you the invitation in the first place."

"We'll remember that," Aahz smiled, his eyes narrowing dangerously.

A thought occurred to me.

"Say . . . um, Lord Chancellor," I said casually, "how did you happen to hear of us in the first place?"

"Why do you ask?" Grimble countered.

"No special reason," I assured him. "But as the interview proved so fruitful, I would like to send a token of my gratitude to that person who spoke so highly of me to you."

It was a pretty flimsy story, but the chancellor seemed to accept it.

"Well . . . um, actually it was a wench," he admitted. "Rather comely, but I don't recall her name just offhand. She may have dyed her hair since you met her. It was green at the time we . . . er . . . met. Do you know her?"

Indeed I did. There was only one woman who knew of Aahz and me, much less our whereabouts. Then again, there was only one woman I knew who fit the description of being voluptuous with green hair. Tanda!

I opened my mouth to acknowledge my recognition, when Aahz dug a warning elbow into my rib.

"Glah!" I said intelligently.

"How's that again?" Grimble inquired.

"I . . . um, I can't place the person, just offhand," I lied. "But you know how absentminded we magicians are."

"Of course," the chancellor smiled, for some reason relieved.

"Now that that's settled," Aahz interrupted, "I believe you mentioned something about our wages."

Grimble scowled for a moment, then broke into a good-natured grin.

"I can see why Master Skeeve leaves his business dealings to you, Aahz," he conceded.

"Flattery's nice," Aahz observed, "but you can't spend it. The subject was our wages."

"You must realize we are a humble kingdom," Grimble sighed, "though we try to reward our retainers as best we can. There have been quarters set aside for the court magician which should be spacious enough to accommodate both of you. Your meals will be provided . . . that is, of course, assuming you are on time when they are served. Also, there is a possibility . . . no, I'd go so far as to say it is a certainty that His Majesty's generosity will be extended to include free stable space and food for your unicorns. How does that sound?"

"So far, pretty cheap," Aahz observed bluntly.

"What do you mean, 'cheap?' " the chancellor snarled, losing his composure for a moment.

"What you've offered so far," Aahz sneered, "is a room we won't be sleeping in, meals we won't be eating, and stable space we won't be using because we'll be in the field fighting your war for you. In exchange, you want Skeeve here to use his skills to save your kingdom. By my calculations, that's cheap!"

"Yes, I see your point," Grimble conceded. "Well, there will, of course, be a small wage paid."

"How small?" Aahz pressed.

"Sufficient to cover your expenses," the chancellor smiled. "Shall we say fifty gold pieces a month?"

"Let's say two hundred," Aahz smiled back.

"Perhaps we could go as high as seventy-five," Grimble countered.

"And we'll come down to two-twenty-five," Aahz offered.

"Considering his skills, we could pay . . . excuse me," the chancellor blinked. "Did you say two-twenty-five?"

"Actually," Aahz conceded, "I misspoke."

"I thought so." Grimble smiled.

"I meant two-fifty."

"Now see here—" the chancellor began.

"Look, Grimble," Aahz met him halfway, "you had three choices. You could double the size of your army, hire a magician, or lose the kingdom. Even at three hundred a month, Skeeve here is your best deal. Don't look at what you're spending, look at what you're saving."

Grimble thought about it for a few moments.

"Very well," he said, grimacing. "Two-fifty it is."

"I believe the figure under discussion was three hundred," I observed pointedly.

That earned me a black look, but I stood my ground and returned his stare levelly.

"Three hundred," he said, forcing the words out through gritted teeth.

"Payable in advance," Aahz added.

"Payable at the end of the pay period," Grimble corrected.

"C'mon, Grimble," Aahz began, but the chancellor interrupted him, holding up his hand.

"No! On that point I must remain inflexible," he insisted. "Everyone in the Royal Retinue is paid at the same time, when the vaults are opened at the end of the pay period. If we break that rule and start allowing exceptions, there will be no end to it."

"Can you at least give us a partial advance?" Aahz pressed. "Something to cover expenses on the upcoming campaign?"

"Definitely not!" Grimble retorted. "If I paid out

monies for services not yet rendered, certain people, specifically Hugh Badaxe, would suspect you intended to take the money and flee without entering battle at all!"

That hit uncomfortably close to home, and I found myself averting my eyes for fear of betraying my guilt. Aahz, however, never even blinked.

"What about bribes?" he asked.

Grimble scowled.

"It is unthinkable that one of the king's retainers would accept a bribe, much less count on it as part of his income. Any attempt to bribe you should be reported immediately to His Majesty!"

"Not *taking* bribes, Grimble," Aahz snarled. "*Giving* them. When we give money out to the enemy, does that come out of our wages, or does the kingdom pay for it?"

"I seriously doubt you could buy off the army facing you," the chancellor observed skeptically. "Besides, you're supposed to carry the day with magik. That's what we're paying you for."

"Even magik is aided by accurate information," Aahz replied pointedly. "C'mon Grimble, you know court intrigue. A little advance warning can go a long way in any battle."

"True enough," the chancellor admitted. "Very well, I guess we can give you an allowance for bribes, assuming it will be kept within reason."

"How much in reason?" Aahz inquired.

"Say . . . five gold pieces."

"Twenty-five would—"

"Five!" Grimble said firmly.

Aahz studied his adversary for a moment, then sighed.

"Five," he said, extending his palm.

The chancellor grudgingly dug into his purse and counted out five gold pieces. In fact, he counted them twice before passing them to Aahz.

"You realize, of course," he warned, "I will require an accounting of those funds after your victory."

"Of course," Aahz smiled, fondling the coins.

"You seem very confident of our victory, Lord Chancellor," I observed.

Grimble regarded me with cocked eyebrow for a moment.

"Of course I am confident, Lord Magician," he said at last. "So confident, I have staked my kingdom, and more importantly, my reputation, on your success. You will note I rate my reputation above the kingdom. That is no accident. Kingdoms rise and fall, but a chancellor can always find employment. That is, of course, providing it was not his advice which brought the kingdom to ruin. Should you fail in your campaign to save Possiltum, my career is finished. If that should happen, gentlemen, your careers fall with mine."

"That has the sound of a threat to it, Grimble," Aahz observed dryly.

"Does it?" the chancellor responded with mock innocence. "That was not my intent. I am not threatening, I am stating a fact. I maintain very close contact with the chancellors of all of the surrounding kingdoms; in fact I am related to several. They are all aware of my position in this magik versus the military issue. Should I prove wrong in my judgment, should you fail in your defense of Possiltum, they will note it. Thereafter, any magician—and you specifically, Skeeve—will be denounced as a fraud and a charlatan should you seek further employment. In fact, as the chancellors frequently control the courts, I would not be surprised if they found an excuse or a trumped-up charge which would allow them to have you put to death as a favor to me. The method of death varies from kingdom to kingdom, but the end result is the same. I trust you will keep that in mind as you plan your campaign."

With that, he turned on his heel and strode away, leaving us standing in silence.

"Well, Aahz," I said finally, "do you have any sound advice on our situation now?"

"Of course," he retorted.

"What?" I asked.

"Now that we've got the whole story," he said solemnly, "now you can panic."

Chapter Nine:

"There is more at stake here than our lives."

—COL. TRAVIS
Alamo Pep Talk

ON the third night after leaving Possiltum's capital, we camped on a small knoll overlooking the kingdom's main north-south trail.

Actually, I use the phase "north-south" rather loosely in this instance. In three days' travel, our progress was the only northward movement we had observed on this particular strip of beaten dirt. The dearth of northbound traffic was emphasized by the high volume of people bound in the opposite direction.

As we traveled we were constantly encountering small groups and families picking their way steadily toward the capital in that unhurried yet ground-eating pace that typifies people accustomed to traveling without means of transport other than their feet. They did not seem particularly frightened or panicky, but two common characteristics marked them all as being more than casual travelers.

First, the great amount of personal effects they carried was far in excess of that required for a simple pilgrimage. Whether bound in cumbersome backpacks or heaped in small, hand-pushed carts, it was obvious the southbound travelers were bringing with them as much of their worldly possessions as they could carry or drag.

Second, no one paid us any heed other than a passing glance. This was even more noteworthy than the prior observation.

Currently, our party consisted of three: myself, Aahz, and Gleep. We had left Buttercup at the palace, much to Aahz's disgust. He would have preferred to leave Gleep and bring Buttercup, but the royal orders had been firm on this point. The dragon was not to remain at the palace unless one or both of us also stayed behind to handle him. As a result, we traveled as a trio—a youth, a dragon, and a grumbling demon—not exactly a common sight in these or any other parts. The peasants flowing south, however, barely noticed us other than to give us clear road space when we passed.

Aahz maintained that this was because whatever they were running from inspired such fear that they barely noted anything or anybody in their path. He further surmised that the motivating force for this exodus could only be the very army we were on our way to oppose.

To prove his point, we attempted to question several of the groups when we encountered them. We stopped doing this after the first day due to the similarities of the replies we received. Sample:

Aahz: Hold, stranger! Where are you going?
Answer: To the capital!

Aahz: Why?

Answer: To be as near as possible to the king when he makes his defense against the invaders from the North. He'll have to try to save himself even if he won't defend the outlands.

Aahz: Citizen you need flee no more. You have underestimated your king's concern for your safety. You see before you the new court magician, retained by His Majesty specifically for the purpose of defending Possiltum from the invading army. What say you to that?

Answer: One magician?

Aahz: With my own able assistance, of course.

Answer: I'd say you were crazy.

Aahz: Now look—

Answer: No, *you* look, whoever or whatever you are. Meaning no disrespect to this or any other magician, you're fools to oppose that army. Magik may be well and good against an ordinary force, but you aren't going to stop *that* army with one magician . . . or twenty magicians for that matter.

Aahz: We have every confidence—

Answer: Fine, then *you* go north. Me, I'm heading for the capital!

Though this exchange had eventually quelled our efforts to reassure the populace, it had given rise to an argument which was still unresolved as we prepared to sleep on the third night.

"What happened to your plan to take the money and run?" I grumbled.

"Big deal," Aahz shot back. "Five whole gold pieces."

"You said you wanted a profit," I pressed.
"Okay! We've got one. So it's small . . . but so was
the effort we put into it. Considering we didn't spend
anything—"

"What about the unicorn?" Aahz countered.
"While they're still holding the unicorn, we've lost
money on the deal."

"Aahz," I reminded him. "Buttercup didn't cost
us anything, remember? He was a gift from Quigley."

"It would cost money to replace him," Aahz insisted. "That means that we lost money on the deal
unless we get him back. I've told you, I want a profit
. . . and definitely refuse to accept a loss."

"Gleep?"

Aahz's heated words had awakened my dragon,
who raised his head in sleepy inquiry.

"Go back to sleep, Gleep!" I said soothingly.
"Everything's all right."

Reassured, he rolled onto his back and laid back
his head.

Ridiculous as he looked, lying there with his four
legs sticking up in the air, he had reminded me of
something.

I pondered the memory for a moment, then decided to change my tactics.

"Aahz," I said thoughtfully, "what's the real
reason for your wanting to go through with this?"

"Weren't you listening, kid? I said—"

"I know, I know," I interrupted. "You said it was
for the profit. The only thing wrong with that is you
tried to leave Gleep behind, who cost us money, instead of Buttercup, who didn't cost us anything!
That doesn't ring true if you're trying to show a
profit with the least possible effort."

"Um, you know how I feel about that stupid dragon—" Aahz began.

"And you know how I feel about him," I interrupted, "As such, you also know I'd never abandon him to save my own skin, much less for money. For some reason, you wanted to be sure I'd see this thing through . . . and that reason has nothing at all to do with money. Now, what is it?"

It was Aahz's turn to lapse into thoughtful silence.

"You're getting better at figuring things out, kid," he said finally.

Normally, I would have been happy to accept the compliment. This time, however, I saw it as what it was: an attempt to distract me.

"The reason, Aahz," I said firmly.

"There are several reasons, kid," he said with uncharacteristic solemnity. "The main one is that you're not a master magician yet."

"If you don't mind my saying so," I commented dryly, "that doesn't make a whole lot of sense. If I'm short on ability, why are you so eager to shove me into this mission?"

"Hear me out, kid," Aahz said, raising a restraining hand. "I made a mistake, and that mistake has dumped us into a situation that needs a master magician. More than a master magician's abilities, we need a master magician's conscience. Do you follow me?"

"No," I admitted.

"Not surprising," Aahz sighed. "That's why I tried to trick you into completing this mission instead of explaining it. So far, all your training has been on physical abilities without developing your professional conscience."

"You've taught me to keep one eye on the

profits," I pointed out defensively.

"That's not what I mean, kid. Look, for a minute forget about profits."

"Are you feeling okay, Aahz?" I asked with genuine concern. "You don't sound like yourself at all."

"Will you get off my back, kid," he snarled. "I'm trying to explain something important!"

I sank into a cowed silence. Still I was reassured. Aahz was definitely Aahz.

"When you were apprenticed to Garkin," Aahz began, "and even when you first met me, you didn't want to be a magician. You wanted to be a thief. To focus your energies behind your lessons, I had to stress how much benefit you could reap from learning magik."

He paused. I didn't say anything. There was nothing to say. He was right, both in his recollections and his interpretation of them.

"Well," he sighed, "there's another side to magik. There's a responsibility . . . a responsibility to your fellow practitioners, and, more importantly, to magik itself. Even though we have rivals and will probably acquire more if we live that long, and even though we may fight with them or beat them out for a job, we are all bound by a common cause. Every magician has a duty to promote magik, to see that its use is respected and reputable. The greater the magician, the greater his sense of duty."

"What's that got to do with our current situation?" I prompted.

"There's an issue at stake here, kid," he answered carefully. "You heard it from Badaxe and Grimble both. More importantly, you heard it from the populace when we talked to the peasants. Rodrick is gambling his entire kingdom on the ability of magik to do a job. Now, no one but a magician can tell how reasonable or unreasonable a task that might be. If we fail, all the laymen will see is that magik failed, and they'll never trust it again. That's why we can't walk away from this mission. We're here representing magik . . . and we've got to give it our best shot.''

I thought about that for a few moments.

"But what can we do against a whole army?" I asked finally.

"To be honest with you," Aahz sighed, "I really don't know. I'm hoping we can come up with an idea after we've seen exactly what it is we're up against.''

We sat silently together for a long time after that, each lost in his own thoughts of the mission and what was at stake.

Chapter Ten:

*"One need not fear superior numbers if
the opposing force has been properly
scouted and appraised."*

—S. BULL

MY last vestige of hope was squashed when we finally
sighted the army. Reports of its massive size had not
been overstated; if anything, they had failed to express the full impact of the force's might.

Our scouting mission had taken us across Possiltum's northern border and several days' journey into
its neighbor's interior. The name of this kingdom
was inconsequential. If it was not already considered
part of the new empire, it would be as soon as the
news spread.

We weren't sure if we had just missed the last
battle, or if the kingdom had simply surrendered.
Whichever the case, there were no defending troops
in evidence, just large encampments of the Empire's
forces spread out in a rough line which disappeared
over the horizon in either direction.

Fortunately, the army was not currently on the
move, which made our scouting considerably easier.

There were sentries posted at regular intervals all along the front line, but as they were not more than a given distance from the encampments, we simply traversed the line without approaching them too closely, and thus escaped detection.

Periodically, we would creep closer to an encampment or climb a tree to improve our view. Aahz seemed very absorbed in his own thoughts, both when we were actually viewing the troops and as we were traveling to new locations. Since I couldn't get more than an occasional grunt or monosyllable out of him, I occupied myself making my own observations.

The soldiers were clothed roughly the same. Standard equipment seemed to include a leather helmet and breastplate, a rough knee-length cloth tunic, sandals, sword, two javelins, and a large rectangular shield. Apparently they were not planning to move immediately, for they had pitched their tents and spent most of their time sharpening weapons, repairing armor, eating, or simply lolling about. Occasionally, a metal-encrusted soldier, presumably an officer, would appear and shout at the others, whereupon they would listlessly form ranks and drill. Their practice would usually grind to a halt as soon as the officer passed from view.

There were occasional pieces of siege equipment designed to throw large rocks or spears long distances, though we never saw them in operation. The only pieces of equipment that seemed to be used with any regularity were the signal towers. Each encampment had one of these, a rickety affair of lashed together poles stretching roughly twenty feet in the air and surmounted by a small, square platform. Several times a day, one soldier in each encampment would mount one of these structures, and they would signal to each other with pennants or standards. The towers also did duty as clotheslines, and were periodically draped with drying tunics.

All in all, it looked like an incredibly boring existence. In fact, from my appraisal, the only thing duller than being a soldier of the Empire was spending days on end watching soldiers of the Empire!

I commented on this to Aahz as we lay belly-down on a grassy knoll, surveying yet another encampment.

"You're right, kid," he admitted absently. "Being a soldier is pretty dull work."

"How about us?" I probed, eager to keep him talking. "What we're doing isn't exactly exciting, you know!"

"You want excitement?" he asked, focusing on me for the first time in days. "Tell you what. Why don't you just stroll down there and ask the Officer of the Day for a quick rundown on how their army operates? I bet that'll liven things up for you."

"I'm not *that* bored!" I amended hastily.

"Then what say you just keep quiet and let me do this my way." Aahz smiled and resumed his studies.

"Do what your way?" I persisted. "Exactly what is it we're trying to accomplish anyway?"

Aahz sighed.

"We're scouting the enemy," he explained patiently. "We've got enough going against us on this campaign without rushing in uninformed."

"How much information do we need?" I grumbled. "This encampment doesn't look any different from the last five we looked at."

"That's because you don't know what you're looking for," Aahz scoffed. "What have you learned so far about the opposition?''

I wasn't ready for the question but I gamely rose to the challenge.

"Um . . . there are a lot of them . . . they're well armed . . . um . . . and they have catapults . . .''

"That's all?" Aahz sneered. "Brilliant! You and Badaxe make a great team of tacticians.''

"Okay, so teach me!" I shot back. "What have you learned?''

"You can spend years trying to learn military theory without scratching the surface,'' my mentor replied sternly. "But I'll try to give you the important parts in a nutshell. To appraise a force, such as we're doing now, remember two words: 'Sam' and 'Doc.' ''

" 'Sam' and 'Doc,' '' I repeated dutifully.

"Some folks prefer to remember 'Salute' but I like 'Sam' and 'Doc,' '' Aahz added as an aside.

"Terrific," I said, grimacing. "Now tell me what it means.''

"They're to help you remember an information checklist," Aahz confided. " 'Salute's stands for Size, Activity, Location, Unit, Time, and Equipment. That's fine as far as it goes, but it assumes no judgmental ability on the part of the scout. I prefer 'Sam' and 'Doc.' That stands for Strength, Armament, Movement, and Deployment, Organization, and Communications.''

"Oh," I said, hoping he wasn't expecting me to remember all this.

"Now, using that framework," Aahz continued, "let's summarize what we've seen so far. Size: there are lots of them, enough so it's kind of pointless to try for an exact count. Movement: currently, they're just sitting there.''

"I got that far all by myself," I pointed out sarcastically.

"The big key, however," Aahz continued, ignoring me, "is in their Armament and Equipment. When you look at this, consider both what is there and what isn't."

"How's that again?" I asked.

"What there is is a lot of foot-schloggers, infantry, a little artillery in the form of catapults and archers, but nothing even vaguely resembling cavalry. That means they're going to go slow when they move, particularly in battle. We don't have to worry about any fast, flanking moves; it'll be a toe-to-toe slugfest."

"But, Aahz—" I began.

"As to the Deployment and Organization," he pushed on undaunted, "they're strung out all over the place, probably because it's easier to forage for food that way. Then again, it displays a certain confidence on their part that they don't feel it's necessary to mass their forces. I think we're looking at their Organization, a collection of companies or battalions each under the leadership of two or three officers, all under the guidance of a super-leader or general."

"Aahz—" I tried again.

"Communications seems to be their most vulnerable point," Aahz pushed on doggedly. "If an army this size doesn't coordinate its movements, it's in big trouble. If they're really using signal towers and runners to pass messages, we might be able to jinx the works for them."

"All of which means what?" I interrupted finally.

"Hmm? Oh, that's a capsule summary of what we're up against," Aahz replied innocently.

"I know. I know," I sighed. "But for days you've been saying you'll formulate a plan after you've seen

what we're up against. Well, you've seen it. What's
the plan? How can we beat 'em?''

"There's no way, kid," Aahz admitted heavily.
"If I had seen one, I would have told you, but I
haven't, and that's why I keep looking."

"Maybe there isn't one," I suggested cautiously.

Aahz sighed.

"I'm starting to think you're right. If so, that
means we'll have to do something I really don't want
to do."

"You mean give up?" I said, genuinely startled.
"After that big speech you gave me about responsibility and—"

"Whoa," Aahz interrupted. "I didn't say anything about giving up. What we're going to do is—"

"Gleep!"

The unmistakable sound came to us from behind,
rolling up the hill from the brush-filled gully where
we'd left my pet.

"Kid," Aahz moaned, "will you keep that stupid
dragon quiet? All we need now is to have him pull the
army down our necks."

"Right, Aahz!" I agreed, worming away backward as fast as I could.

As soon as I was clear of the crest of the hill, I rose
to a low crouch and scuttled down the slope in that
position. Crawling is neither a fast nor comfortable
means of travel for me.

As per our now normal procedure, we had tethered
Gleep to a tree . . . a large tree after he had success-
fully uprooted several small ones. Needless to say, he
wasn't wild about the idea, but it was necessary considering the delicate nature of our current work.

"Gleep!"

I could see him now, eagerly straining at the end of

his rope. Surprisingly, however, for a change he wasn't trying to get to me. In fact, he was trying his best to get at a large bush which stood some distance from his tree . . . or at something hidden in the bush!

Cold sweat suddenly popped out on my brow. It occurred to me that Gleep might have been discovered by one of the enemy army scouts. That would be bad enough, but even worse was the possibility said scout might still be around.

I hurriedly stepped sideways into the shadow of a tree and reviewed the situation. I hadn't actually *seen* a scout. In fact, there was no movement at all in the indicated bush. I could sneak back and get Aahz, but if I were wrong he wouldn't be very happy over being called to handle a false alarm. I could set Gleep loose and let him find the intruder, but that would mean exposing myself.

As I stood debating my next course of action, someone slipped up behind me and put hands over my eyes.

"Surprise!" came a soft voice in my ear.

Chapter Eleven:

*"Should old acquaintance be for-
got. . . ."*
—COUNT OF MONTE CRISTO

I JUMPED!

Perhaps I should clarify. When I say "I jumped,"
I mean I really jumped. Over a year ago, Aahz had
taught me to fly, which is actually controlled hovering caused by reverse levitation.

Whatever it was, I did it. I went straight up in the
air about ten feet and stayed there. I didn't know
what had snuck up behind me, and didn't want to
know. I wanted help! I wanted Aahz!

I drew a mighty breath to express this desire.

"Kinda jumpy, aren't you, handsome?"

That penetrated my panic.

Stifling my shout before it truly began, I looked
down on my attacker. From my vantage point, I was
treated to a view of a gorgeous golden-olive complex-
ioned face, accented by almond-shaped cat's eyes,
framed by a magnificent tumble of light green hair. I
could also see a generous expanse of cleavage.

"Tanda!" I crowed with delight, forcing my eyes back to her face.

"Do you mind coming down?" she called. "I can't come up."

I considered swooping down on her dramatically, but decided against it. I'm still not all that good at flying, and the effect would be lost completely if I crashed into her.

Instead, I settled for lowering myself gently to the ground a few paces from her.

"Gee, Tanda, I . . . *glack!*"

The last was squeezed forcefully from me as she swept me into a bone-crushing embrace.

"Gee, it's good to see you, handsome," she murmured happily. "How have you been?"

"I *was* fine," I noted, untangling myself briefly. "What are you doing here?"

The last time I had seen her, Tanda was part of the ill-fated group Aahz and I had seen off to dimensions unknown. Of the whole crowd, she had been the only one I was sorry to see go.

"I'm waiting for you, silly," she teased, slipping an affectionate arm around my waist. "Where's Aahz?"

"He's—" I started to point up the hill when a thought occurred to me. "Say . . . how did you know I had Aahz with me?"

"Oh! Don't get mad," she scolded, giving me a playful shake. "It stands to reason. Even Aahz wouldn't let you face that army alone."

"But how did you—"

"Gleep!"

My dragon had discovered his quarry was no longer hiding behind the bush. As a result, he was now straining at the end of his rope trying to reach

us. The tree he was tethered to was swaying dangerously.

"Gleep!" Tanda called in a delighted voice. "How
are ya, fella?"

The tree dipped to new lows as my dragon quivered
with glee at having been recognized. I was quivering a
little myself. Tanda had that affect on males.

Heedless of her own safety, Tanda bounded forward to kneel before the dragon, pulling his whiskers
and scratching his nose affectionately.

Gleep loved it. I loved it, too. In addition to her
usual soft, calf-high boots, Tanda was wearing a
short green tunic which hugged her generous curves
and showed off her legs just swell. What's more,
when she knelt down like that, the hem rode up
until. . . .

"What's wrong with that dragon?" Aahz boomed,
bursting out of the brush behind me.

This time I didn't jump . . . much.

"Gee, Aahz," I began. "It's . . ."

I needn't have bothered trying to explain.

Tanda uncoiled and came past me in a bound.

"Aahz!" she exclaimed, flinging herself into his
arms.

For a change, my mentor was caught as flat-footed
as I had been. For a moment, the tangle of arms
teetered on the brink of collapse, then down it went.

They landed with a resounding thump, Aahz on
the bottom and therefore soaking up most of the impact.

"Still impulsive, aren't you?" Tanda leered.

"Whoosh . . . hah . . . ah . . ." Aahz responded ur-
banely.

Tanda rolled to her feet and began rearranging her
tunic.

"At least I don't have to ask if you're glad to see me," she observed.

"Tanda!" Aahz gasped at last.

"You remembered?" Tanda beamed.

"She's been waiting for us, Aahz," I supplied brightly.

"That's right!" Aahz scowled. "Grimble said you set us up for this job."

Tanda winced.

"I can explain that," she said apologetically.

"I can hardly wait," Aahz intoned.

"I'm kind of curious about that myself," I added.

"Um . . . this could take a while, guys," she said thoughtfully. "Got anything around to drink?"

That was easily the most reasonable question asked so far today. We broke out the wine, and in no time were sitting around in a small circle quenching our thirst. Much to Aahz's disgust, I insisted we sit close enough to Gleep that he not be left out. This meant, of course, his rather aromatic breath flavored our discussion, but as I pointed out it was the only way to keep him quiet while we talked.

"What happened after you left?" I prodded. "Where are Isstvan and Brockhurst and Higgins? What happened to Quigley? Did they ever bring Frumple back to life, or is he still a statue?"

"Later, kid," Aahz interrupted. "First things first. You were about to explain about Grimble."

"Grimble," Tanda responded, wrinkling her nose. "Did you ever notice the 'crookeder' a person is, the more possessive he is? He's the main reason I didn't wait for you at Possiltum."

"From the beginning," Aahz instructed.

"From the beginning." Tanda pursed her lips thoughtfully. "Well, I picked him up in a singles bar

. . . he's married, but I didn't know that till later.''

"What's a singles bar?" I interrupted.

"Shut up, kid," Aahz snarled.

"Well, it wasn't actually a singles bar," Tanda corrected. "It was more of a tavern. I should have known he was married. I mean, nobody that young is *that* bald unless he's got a wife at home."

"Skip the philosophy," Aahz moaned. "Just tell us the story, huh?"

Tanda cocked an eyebrow at him.

"You know, Aahz," she accused, "for someone as long-winded as you are when it comes to telling stories, you're awfully impatient when it comes to listening to someone else."

"She's right, you know," I commented.

"Enough!" Aahz bellowed. "The story!"

"Well, one of the things Grimble mentioned while he was trying to impress me with how important his job was, was that he was trying to find a court magician. He said he had convinced the king to hire one, but now he couldn't find one and was going to end up looking like an idiot."

"And when he mentioned idiots," I supplied, "naturally you thought of us."

"Now, don't be that way," Tanda scolded. "I thought it was a good way to help out a couple of friends. I knew you two were hanging out in this neck of the woods . . . and everybody knows what a cushy job being a court magician is."

"What did I tell you, kid," Aahz commented.

"We must be talking about different jobs," I retorted.

"Hey," Tanda interrupted, laying a soft hand on my arm. "When I gave him your names, I didn't know about the invading army. Honest!"

My anger melted away at her touch. Right then, she could have told me she had sold my head as a centerpiece and I would have forgiven her.

"Well . . ." I began, but she persisted, which was fine by me.

"As soon as I found out what the real story was, I knew I had gotten you into a tight spot," she said with soft sincerity. "Like I said, I would have waited at Possiltum, but I was afraid what with your disguises and all, that you'd recognize me before I spotted you. If you gave me the kind of greeting I've grown to expect, it could have really queered the deal. Grimble's a jealous twit, and if he thought we were more than nodding acquaintances, he would have held back whatever support he might normally give."

"Big deal," Aahz grumbled. "Five whole gold pieces."

"That much?" Tanda sounded honestly surprised. "Which arm did you break?"

"Aahz always gets us the best possible deal," I said proudly. "At least, monetarily."

"Well," Tanda concluded, "at least I won't dig into your war funds. When I found out the mess I had gotten you into, I decided I'd work this one for free. Since I got you into it, the least I can do is help get you out."

"That's terrific," I exclaimed.

"It sure is!" Aahz agreed.

Something in his voice annoyed me.

"I meant that she was helping us," I snarled. "Not that she was doing it for free."

"That's what I meant, too, apprentice," Aahz glowered back. "But unlike some, I know what I'm talking about!"

"Boys, boys," Tanda said, separating us with her hands. "We're on the same side. Remember?"

"Gleep!" said the dragon, siding with Tanda.

As I have said, Gleep's breath is powerful enough to stop any conversation, and it was several minutes before the air cleared enough for us to continue.

"Before we were so rudely interrupted," Tanda gasped at last, "you were starting to say something, Aahz. Have you got a plan?"

"Now I do," Aahz smiled, chucking her under the chin. "And believe me, doing it without you would have been rough."

That had an anxious sound to it. Tanda's main calling, at least the only one mentionable in polite company, was Assassin.

"C'mon, Aahz," I chided. "Tanda's good, but she's not good enough to take on a whole army."

"Don't bet on it, handsome," she corrected, winking at me.

I blushed but continued with my argument.

"I still say the job's too big for one person, or three people for that matter," I insisted.

"You're right, kid," Aahz said solemnly.

"We just can't . . . what did you say, Aahz?"

"I said you were right," Aahz repeated.

"I thought so," I marveled. "I just wanted to hear it again."

"You'd *hear* it more often if you were *right* more often," Aahz pointed out.

"C'mon, Aahz," Tanda interrupted. "What's the plan?"

"Like the kid says," Aahz said loftily, "we need more help. We need an army of our own."

"But Aahz," I reminded him, "Badaxe said—"

"Who said anything about Badaxe?" Aahz replied

innocently. "We're supposed to win this war with magik, aren't we? Well, fine. With Tanda on our team, we've got a couple of extra skills to draw on. Remember?"

I remembered. I remembered Aahz saying he wasn't worried about Tanda leaving with Isstvan because she could travel the dimensions by herself if things got rough. The light began to dawn.

"You mean . . ."

"That's right, kid," Aahz smiled. "We're going back to Deva. We're going to recruit a little invasionary force of our own!"

Chapter Twelve:

"This is no game for old men! Send in the boys!"

—W. Hays

I DON'T know how Tanda transported us from Klah to Deva. If I did, we wouldn't have needed her. All I know is that at the appropriate time she commenced to chant and shift her shoulders (a fascinating process in itself), and we were there.

"There," in this case, was at the Bazaar at Deva. That phrase alone, however, does not begin to describe our new surroundings as they came into focus.

A long time ago, the dimension of Deva had undergone an economic collapse. To survive, the Deveels (who I once knew as devils) used their ability to travel the dimensions and become merchants. Through the process of natural selection, the most successful Deveels were not the best fighters, but the best traders. Now, after countless generations of this process, the Deveels were acknowledged as the best merchants in all the dimensions. They were also acknowledged as being the shrewdest, coldest, most profit-hungry cheats ever to come down the pike.

The Bazaar at Deva was their showcase. It was an all-day, all-night, year-round fair where the Deveels met to haggle with each other over the wares fetched back from the various dimensions. Though it was originally established and maintained by Deveels, it was not unusual to find travelers from many dimensions shopping the endless rows of displays and booths. The rule of thumb was, "If it's to be found anywhere, you'll find it at the Bazaar at Deva."

I had been here once before with Aahz. At the time, we were searching for a surprise weapon to use against Isstvan. What we ended up with was Gleep and Tanda! . . . Distractions abound at the Bazaar.

I mention this in part to explain why, as unusual as our foursome must have appeared, no one paid us the slightest attention as we stood watching the kaleidoscope of activity whirling about us.

Gleep pressed against me for reassurance, momentarily taken aback at the sudden change of surroundings. I ignored him. My first visit to this place had been far too brief for my satisfaction. As such, I was rubbernecking madly, trying to see as much as possible as fast as possible.

Tanda was more businesslike.

"Now that we're here, Aahz," she drawled, "do you know where we're going?"

"No," Aahz admitted. "But I'll find out right now."

Without further warning, he casually reached out and grabbed the arm of the nearest passerby, a short, ugly fellow with tusks. Spinning his chosen victim around, Aahz bent to scowl in his face.

"You!" he snarled. "Do you like to fight?"

For a moment my heart stopped. All we needed now was to get into a brawl.

Fortunately, instead of producing a weapon, the tusker gave ground a step and eyed our party suspiciously.

"Not with a Pervert backed by a dragon, I don't," he retorted cautiously.

"Good!" Aahz smiled. "Then if you wanted to hire someone to do your fighting for you, where would you go?"

"To the Bazaar at Deva," the tusker shrugged.

"I know that!" Aahz snarled. "But *where* at the Bazaar?"

"Oh," the tusker exclaimed with sudden understanding. "About twenty rows in that direction, then turn right for another thirty or so. That's where the mercenaries hang out."

"Twenty, then up thirty," Aahz repeated carefully. "Thanks."

"A finder's fee would be appreciated more than any thanks," the tusker smiled, extending a palm.

"You're right!" Aahz agreed, and turned his back on our benefactor.

The tusker hesitated for a moment, then shrugged and continued on his way. I could have told him that Perverts in general and Aahz specifically are not noted for their generosity. "We go twenty rows that way, then up thirty," Aahz informed us.

"Yeah, we heard," Tanda grimaced. "Why didn't you just ask him flat out?"

"My way is quicker," Aahz replied smugly.

"Is it?" I asked skeptically.

"Look kid," Aahz scowled. "Do you want to lead us through this zoo?"

"Well . . ." I hesitated.

"Then shut up and let me do it, okay?"

Actually, I was more than willing to let Aahz lead the way to wherever it was we were going. For one thing, it kept him busy navigating a path through the crowd. For another, it left me with next to nothing to do except marvel at the sights of the Bazaar as I followed along in his wake.

Try as I might, though, there was just too much for one set of eyes to see.

In one booth, two Deveels argued with an elephant-headed being over a skull; at least, I think it was a skull. In another, a Deveel was putting on a demonstration for a mixed group of shoppers, summoning clouds of floating green bubbles from a tiny wooden box.

At one point, our path was all but blocked by a booth selling rings which shot bolts of lightning. Between the salesman's demonstrations and the customers trying out their purchases, the way was virtually impassable.

Aahz and Tanda never broke stride, however, confidently maintaining their pace as they walked through the thick of the bolts. Miraculously, they passed through unscathed.

Gritting my teeth, I seized one of Gleep's ears and followed in their footsteps. Again, the bolts of energy failed to find us. Apparently no Deveel would bring injury or allow anyone in his shop to bring injury to a potential customer. It was a handy fact to know.

The lightning rings brought something else to mind, however. The last time we parted company with Tanda, Aahz had given her a ring that shot a heat ray capable of frying a man-sized target on the spot. That's right . . . I said he *gave* it to her. You might think this was proof of the depth of his feelings for her. It's my theory he was sick. Anyway, I was reminded of the ring and curious as to what had become of it.

Increasing my pace slightly, I closed the distance between myself and the pair in the lead, only to find they were already deeply engrossed in conversation. The din that prevails at the Bazaar stymies any attempt at serious eavesdropping, but I managed to catch occasional bits and pieces of the conversation as we walked.

". . . heard . . . awfully expensive, aren't they?" Tanda was saying.

". . . lick their weight in . . ." Aahz replied smugly.

I moved in a little closer, trying to hear better.

". . . makes you think they've got anyone here?" Tanda asked.

"With the number of bars here?" Aahz retorted. "The way I hear it, this is one of their main . . ."

I lost the rest of that argument. A knee-high, tentacled mass suddenly scuttled across my boots and ducked through a tent flap, closely pursued by two very frustrated-looking Deveels.

I ignored the chase and the following screams, hurrying to catch up with Aahz and Tanda again. Apparently they were discussing mercenaries, and I wanted to hear as much as possible, both to further my education, and because I might have to lead them into battle eventually.

". . . find them?" Tanda was asking. "All we have is a general area."

". . . easy," Aahz replied confidently. "Just listen for the singing."

"Singing?" Tanda was skeptical.

"It's their trademark," Aahz pronounced. "It also lands them in most of their . . ."

A Deveel stepped in front of me, proudly displaying a handful of seeds. He threw them on the ground with a flourish, and a dense black thornbush sprang up to block my path. Terrific. Normally, I would have been fascinated, but at the moment I was in a hurry.

Without even pausing to upbraid the Deveel, I took to the air, desperation giving wings to my feet . . . desperation assisted by a little levitation. I cleared the thornbush easily, touched down lightly on the far side, and was practically trampled by Gleep as he burst through the barrier.

"Gleep?" he said, cocking his head at me curiously.

I picked myself up from the dust where I had been knocked by his enthusiasm and cuffed him.

"Watch where you're going next time," I ordered angrily.

He responded by snaking out his long tongue and licking my face. His breath was devastating and his tongue left a trail of slime. Obviously my admonishment had terrified him.

Heaving a deep sigh, I sprinted off after Aahz with Gleep lumbering along in hot pursuit.

I was just overtaking them when Aahz stopped suddenly in his tracks and started to turn. Unable to halt my headlong sprint, I plowed into him, knocking him sprawling.

"In a hurry, handsome?" Tanda asked, eyeing me slyly.

"Gee, Aahz," I stammered, bending over him, "I didn't mean to—"

From a half sitting position, his hand lashed out in

a cuff that spun me halfway around.

"Watch where you're going next time," he growled.

"Gleep!" said the dragon and licked my face.

Either my head was spinning more than I thought, or I had been through this scene before.

"Now quit clowning around and listen, kid."

Aahz was on his feet again, and all business.

"Here's where we part company for a while. You wait here while I go haggle with the mercenaries."

"Gee, Aahz," I whined. "Can't I—"

"No, you can't!" he said firmly. "The crew I'm going after is sharp. All we need is one of your dumb questions in the middle of negotiations and they'll triple their prices."

"But—" I began.

"You will wait here," Aahz ordered. "I repeat, *wait*. No fights, no window shopping for dragons, just wait!"

"I'll stay here with him, Aahz," Tanda volunteered.

"Good," Aahz nodded. "And try to keep him out of trouble, okay?"

With that, he turned and disappeared into the crowd. Actually, I wasn't too disappointed. I mean, I would have liked to have gone with him, but I liked having some time alone with Tanda even more . . . that is, if you can consider standing in the middle of the Bazaar at Deva being alone with someone.

"Well, Tanda," I said, flashing my brightest smile.

"Later, handsome," she replied briskly. "Right now I've got some errands to run."

"Errands?" I blinked.

"Yeah. Aahz is big on manpower, but I'd just as

soon have a few extra tricks up my sleeve in case the going gets rough," she explained. "I'm going to duck over to the special effects section and see what they have in stock."

"Okay," I agreed. "Let's go."

"No, you don't," she said, shaking her head. "I think I'd better go this one alone. The kind of places I have in mind aren't fit for civilized customers. You and the dragon wait here."

"But you're supposed to be keeping me out of trouble!" I argued.

"And that's why I'm not taking you along," she said, smiling. "Now, what do you have along in the way of weaponry?"

"Well . . ." I said hesitantly, "there's a sort of a sword in one of Gleep's packs."

"Fine!" she said. "Get it out and wear it. It'll keep the riffraff at a distance. Then . . . um . . . wait for me in there!"

She pointed at a strange-looking stone structure with a peeling sign on its front.

"What is it?" I asked, peering at it suspiciously.

"It's a 'Yellow Crescent Inn,' " she explained. "It's sort of a restaurant. Get yourself something to eat. The food's unappetizing, but vaguely digestible."

I studied the place for a moment.

"Actually," I decided finally, "I think I'd rather . . ."

Right about there I discovered I was talking to myself. Tanda had disappeared without a trace.

For the second time in my life I was alone in the Bazaar at Deva.

Chapter Thirteen:

"Hold the pickles, hold the lettuce."
—HENRY VIII

FASCINATING as the Bazaar is, facing it alone can be rather frightening.

Being particularly susceptible to fear, I decided to follow Tanda's advice and entered the inn.

First, however, I took the precaution of tethering Gleep to the inn's hitching post and unpacking the sword. We had one decent sword. Unfortunately, Aahz was currently wearing it. That left me with Garkin's old sword, a weapon which has been sneered at by demon and demon-hunter alike. Still, its weight was reassuring on my hip, though it might have been more reassuring if I had known anything about how to handle it. Unfortunately, my lessons with Aahz to date had not included swordsmanship. I could only hope it would not be apparent to the casual observer that this was my first time to wear a sword.

Pausing in the door, I surveyed the inn's interior. Unaccustomed as I was to gracious dining, I realized in a flash that this wasn't it.

One of the few pieces of advice my farmer father had given me before I ran away from home was not to trust any inn or restaurant that appeared overly clean. He maintained the cleaner a place was, the more dubious the quality and origin of their food would be. If he were even vaguely right, this inn must be the bottom of the barrel. It was not only clean, it gleamed.

I do not mean that figuratively. Harsh overhead lights glinted off a haphazard arrangement of tiny tables and uncomfortable-looking chairs constructed of shiny metal and a hard white substance I didn't recognize. At the far end of the inn was a counter behind which stood a large stone gargoyle, the only decorative feature in the place. Behind the gargoyle was a door, presumably leading into the kitchen. There was a small window in the door through which I caught glimpses of the food being prepared. Preparation consisted of passing patties of meat over a stove, cramming them into a split roll, slopping a variety of colored pastes on top of the meat, and wrapping the whole mess in a piece of paper.

Watching this process confirmed my earlier fears. I do all the cooking for Aahz and myself, as I did before that for Garkin and myself, and before that just for myself. While I have no delusions as to the high quality of my cooking, I do know that what they were doing to that meat could only yield a meal the consistency and flavor of charred glove leather.

Despite the obvious low quality of the food, the inn seemed nearly full of customers. I noticed this out of the corner of my eye. I also noticed that a high percentage of them were staring at me. It occurred to me that this was probably because I had been standing in the door for some time without entering while working up my courage to go in.

Feeling slightly embarrassed, I stepped inside and let the door swing shut behind me. With fiendish accuracy, the door closed on my sword, pinning it momentarily and forcing me to break stride clumsily as I started forward. So much for my image as a swordsman.

Humiliated, I avoided looking at the other customers and made my way hurriedly to the inn's counter. I wasn't sure what I was going to do once I got there, since I didn't trust the food, but hopefully people would stop staring at me if I went through the motions of ordering.

Still trying to avoid eye contact with anyone, I made a big show of studying the gargoyle. There was a grinding noise, and the statue turned its head to return my stare. If wasn't a statue! They really had a gargoyle tending the counter!

The gargoyle seemed to be made of coarse gray stone, and when he flexed his wings, small pieces of crushed rock and dust showered silently to the floor. His hands were taloned, and there were curved spikes growing out of his elbows. The only redeeming feature I could see was his smile, which in itself was a bit unnerving. Dominating his wrinkled face, the smile seemed permanently etched in place, stretching well past his ears and displaying a set of pointed teeth even longer than Aahz's.

"Take your order?" the gargoyle asked politely, the smile never twitching.

"Um . . ." I said taking a step back. "I'll have to think about it. There's so much to choose from."

In actuality I couldn't read the menu . . . if that's what it was. There was something etched in the wall behind the gargoyle in a language I couldn't decipher. I assume it was a menu because the prices weren't etched in the wall, but written in chalk over many erasures.

The gargoyle shrugged.

"Suit yourself," he said indifferently. "When you make up your mind, just holler. The name's Gus."

"I'll do that . . . Gus," I smiled, backing slowly toward the door.

Though it was my intent to exit quietly and wait outside with Gleep, things didn't work out that way. Before I had taken four steps, a hand fell on my shoulder.

"Skeeve, isn't it?" a voice proclaimed.

I spun around, or started to. I was brought up short when my sword banged into a table leg. My head kept moving, however, and I found myself face to face with an Imp.

"Brockhurst!" I exclaimed, recognizing him immediately.

"I thought I recognized you when you . . . *hey!*" The Imp took a step backward and raised his hands defensively. "Take it easy! I'm not looking for any trouble."

My hand had gone to my sword hilt in an involuntary effort to free it from the table leg. Apparently Brockhurst had interpreted the gesture as an effort to draw my weapon.

That was fine by me. Brockhurst had been one of Isstvan's lieutenants, and we hadn't parted on the best of terms. Having him a little afraid of my "ready sword" was probably a good thing.

"I don't hold any grudges," Brockhurst continued insistently. "That was just a job! Right now I'm between jobs . . . permanently!"

That last was added with a note of bitterness which piqued my curiosity.

"Things haven't been going well?" I asked cautiously.

The Imp grimaced.

"That's an understatement. Come on, sit down. I'll buy you a milkshake and tell you all about it."

I wasn't certain what a milkshake was, but I was sure I didn't want one if they were sold here.

"Um . . . thanks anyway, Brockhurst," I said, forcing a smile, "but I think I'll pass."

The Imp arched an eyebrow at me.

"Still a little suspicious, eh?" he murmured. "Well, can't say as I blame you. Tell you what we'll do."

Before I could stop him, he strolled to the counter.

"Hey, Gus!" he called. "Mind if I take an extra cup?"

"Actually . . ." the gargoyle began.

"Thanks!"

Brockhurst was already on his way back, bearing his prize with him, some kind of a thin-sided, flimsy cannister. Plopping down at a nearby table, he beckoned to me, indicating the seat opposite him with a wave of his hand.

There was no gracious course for me to follow other than to join him, though it would later occur to me I had no real obligation to be gracious. Moving carefully to avoid knocking anything over with my sword, I maneuvered my way to the indicated seat.

Apparently, Brockhurst had been sitting here before, as there was already a cannister on the table identical to the one he had fetched from the counter. The only difference was that the one on the table was three-quarters full of a curious pink liquid.

With great ceremony, the Imp picked up the cannister from the table and poured half its contents into the new vessel. The liquid poured with the consistency of swamp muck.

"Here!" he said, pushing one of the cannisters across the table to me. "Now you don't have to worry about any funny business with the drinks. We're both drinking the same thing."

With that, he raised his vessel in a mock toast and took a healthy swallow from it. Apparently he expected me to do the same. I would have rather sucked blood.

"Um . . . it's hard to believe things aren't going well for you," I stalled. "You look well enough."

For a change, I was actually sincere. Brockhurst looked good . . . even for an Imp. As Aahz had said, Imps are snappy dressers, and Brockhurst was no exception. He was outfitted in a rust-colored velvet jerkin trimmed in gold, which set off his pink complexion and sleek black hair superbly. If he were starving, you couldn't tell it from looking at him. Though still fairly slender, he was as well muscled and adroit as when I had first met him.

"Don't let appearances fool you," Brockhurst insisted, shaking his head. "You see before you an Imp pushed to the wall. I've had to sell everything—my crossbow, my pouch of magic tricks—I couldn't even raise enough money to pay my dues to the Assassins Guild."

"It's that hard to find work?" I sympathized.

"I'll tell you, Skeeve," he whispered confidentially, "I haven't worked since that fiasco with Isstvan."

The sound of that name still sent chills down my back.

"Where is Isstvan, anyway?" I asked casually.

"Don't worry about him," Brochkurst said grimly. "We left him working concession stands on the Isle of Coney, a couple of dimensions from here."

"What happened to the others?"

I was genuinely curious. I hadn't had much of a chance to talk with Tanda since our reunion.

"We left Frumple under a cloud of birds in some park or other . . . figured he looked better as a statue than he did alive. The demon hunter and the girl took off for parts unknown one night while we were asleep. My partner, Higgens, headed back to Imper. He figured his career was over and that he might as well settle down. Me, I've been looking for work ever since, and I'm starting to think Higgens was right."

"Come on, Brockhurst," I chided. "There must be something you can do. I mean, this is the Bazaar."

The Imp heaved a sigh and took another sip of his drink.

"It's nice of you to say that, Skeeve," he smiled. "But I've got to face the facts. There's not a big demand for Imps anyway, and none at all for an Imp with no powers."

I knew what he meant. All the dimension travelers I had met so far—Aahz, Isstvan, Tanda, and even the Deveel Frumple—seemed to regard Imps as inferior beings. The nicest thing I had heard said about them was that they were styleless imitators of the Deveels.

I felt sorry for him. Despite the fact we had first met as enemies, it wasn't that long ago I had been a loser nobody wanted.

"You've got to keep trying," I encouraged.

"Somewhere, there's someone who wants to hire you."

"Not very likely," the Imp grimaced. "The way I am now, *I* wouldn't hire me. Would you?"

"Sure I would," I insisted. "In a minute."

"Oh, well," he sighed. "I shouldn't dwell on myself. How have things been with you? What brings you to the Bazaar?"

Now it was my turn to grimace.

"Aahz and I are in a bad spot," I explained. "We're here trying to recruit a force to help us out."

"You're hiring people?" Brockhurst was suddenly intense.

"Yeah. Why?" I replied.

Too late, I realized what I was saying.

"Then you weren't kidding about hiring me!" Brockhurst was beside himself with glee.

"Um . . ." I said.

"This is great," the Imp chortled, rubbing his hands together. "Believe me, Skeeve, you won't regret this."

I was regretting it already.

"Wait a minute, Brockhurst," I interrupted desperately. "There are a few things you should know about the job."

"Like what?"

"Well . . . for one thing, the odds are bad," I said judiciously. "We're up against an army. That's pretty rough fare considering how low the pay is."

I thought I would touch a nerve with that remark about the pay. I was right.

"How low *is* the pay?" the Imp asked bluntly.

Now I was stuck. I didn't have the vaguest idea how much mercenaries were normally paid.

"We . . . um . . . we couldn't offer you more than

one gold piece for the whole job," I shrugged.

"Done!" Brockhurst proclaimed. "With the current state of my finances, I can't turn down an offer like that no matter how dangerous it is."

It occurred to me that sometime I should have Aahz give me a quick course in rates of exchange.

"Um . . . there's one other problem," I murmured thoughtfully.

"What's that?"

"Well, my partner, you remember Aahz?"

The Imp nodded.

"Well, he's out right now trying to hire a force, and he's got the money," I continued. "There's a good chance that if he's successful, and he usually is, there won't be enough money left to hire you."

Brockhurst pursed his lips for a moment, then shrugged.

"Well," he said, "I'll take the chance. I wasn't going anywhere anyway. As I said, they haven't exactly been beating my door down with job offers."

I had run out of excuses.

"Well"—I smiled lamely—"as long as you're aware—"

"Heads up, boss," the Imp's murmur interrupted me. "We've got company."

I'm not sure which worried me more, Brockhurst calling me "boss" or the specterlike character who had just stepped up to our table.

Chapter Fourteen:

"We're looking for a few good men."
—B. CASSIDY

FOR a moment I thought we were being confronted by a skeleton. Then I looked closer and realized there really *was* skin stretched over the bones, though its dusty-white color made it seem very dead indeed.

The figure's paleness was made even more corpse-like by the blue-black hooded robe that enshrouded it. It wasn't until I noted the wrinkled face with a short, bristly white beard that I realized our visitor was actually a very old man . . . very old.

He looked weak to the point of near collapse, desperately clutching a twisted black walking staff which seemed to be the only thing keeping him erect. Still, his eyes were bright and his smile confident as he stood regarding us.

"Did I hear you boys right?" he asked in a crackling voice.

"I beg your pardon?" Brockhurst scowled at him.

The ancient figure sneered and raised his voice.

"I said, 'Did I hear you boys right?'!" he barked.

"What's the matter? Are you deaf?"

"Um . . . excuse me," I interrupted hastily. "Before we can answer you, we have to know what you thought we said."

The old man thought for a minute, then bobbed his head in a sudden nod.

"You know, yer right!" he cackled. "Pretty smart, young fella."

He began to list, but caught himself before he fell.

"Thought I heard you tell Pinko here you were looking for a force to take on an army," he pronounced, jerking a thumb at Brockhurst.

"The name's Brockhurst, not Pinko!" the Imp snarled.

"All right, Bratwurst," the old man nodded. "No need to get your dander up."

"That's Brockhurst!"

"You heard right," I interrupted again, hoping the old man would go away as soon as his curiosity was satisfied.

"Good!" the man declared. "Count me in! Me and Blackie haven't been in a good fight for a long time."

"How long is that in centuries?" Brockhurst sneered.

"Watch your mouth, Bratwurst!" the old man warned. "We may be old, but we can still teach you a thing or two about winnin' wars."

"Who's Blackie?" I asked, cutting off Brockhurst's reply.

In reply, the old man drew himself erect . . . well, nearly erect, and patted his walking staff.

"This is Blackie!" he announced proudly. "The finest bow ever to come from Archiah, and that takes in a lot of fine bows!"

I realized with a start that the walking staff was a bow, unstrung, with its bowstring wrapped around it. It was unlike any bow I had ever seen, lumpy and uneven, but polished to a sheen that seemed to glimmer with a life all its own.

"Wait a minute!" Brockhurst was suddenly attentive. "Did you say you come from Archiah?"

"That I did," the old man grinned. "Ajax's the name, fighting's my game. Ain't seen a war yet that could lay old Ajax low, and I've seen a lot of 'em."

"Um . . . could you excuse us for just a minute, sir?" Brockhurst smiled apologetically.

"Sure, son," Ajax nodded. "Take your time."

I couldn't understand the Imp's sudden change in attitude, but he seemed quite intense as he jerked his head at me, so I leaned close to hear what he had to say.

"Hire him, boss!" he hissed in my ear.

"What?" I gasped, not believing I had heard him right.

"I said hire him!" the Imp repeated. "I may not have much to offer you, but I can give you advice. Right now, my advice is to hire him."

"But he's—"

"He's from Archiah!" Brockhurst interrupted. "Boss, that dimension *invented* archery. You don't find many genuine Archers of any age for hire. If you've really got a war on your hands, hire him. He could tip the balance for us."

"If he's that good," I whispered back, "can we afford him?"

"One gold piece will be adequate," Ajax smiled toothily, adding his head to our conference. "I accept your offer."

"Excellent!" Brockhurst beamed.

"Wait a minute," I shrieked desperately, "I have a partner that—"

"I know, I know," Ajax sighed, holding up a restraining hand. "I heard when you told Bratwurst here."

"That's Brockhurst," the Imp growled, but he did it smiling.

"If your partner can't find help, then we're hired!" the old man laughed, shaking his head. "It's a mite strange, but these are strange times."

"You can say that again," I muttered.

I was beginning to think I had spoken too loud in my conversation with Brockhurst.

"One thing you should know, though, youngster," Ajax murmured confidentially. "I'm bein' followed."

"By who?" I asked.

"Don't rightly know," he admitted. "Haven't figured it out yet. It's the little blue fella in the corner behind me."

I craned my neck to look at the indicated corner. It was empty.

"What fella? I mean, fellow," I corrected myself.

Ajax whipped his head around with a speed that belied his frail appearance.

"Dang it," he cursed. "He did it again. I'm telling you, youngster, that's why I can't figure what he's after!"

"Ah . . . sure, Ajax," I said soothingly. "You'll catch him next time."

Terrific. An Imp with no powers, and now an old Archer who sees things.

My thoughts were interrupted by a gentle tap on my shoulder. I turned to find the gargoyle looming over me.

"Your order's ready, sir," he said through his perma-smile.

"My order?"

"Yes, if you'll step this way."

"There must be some mistake," I began, "I didn't . . ."

The gargoyle was already gone, lumbering back to his counter. I considered ignoring him. Then I considered his size and countenance, and decided I should straighten out this misunderstanding in a polite fashion.

"Excuse me," I told my charges. "I'll be right back."

"Don't worry about us, boss," Brockhurst waved.

I wasn't reassured.

I managed to make my way to the counter without banging my sword against anything or anyone, a feat that raised my spirits for the first time that afternoon. Thus bolstered, I approached the gargoyle.

"I . . . um . . . I don't recall ordering anything," I stated politely.

"Don't blame you, either," the gargoyle growled through his smile. "Beats me how anyone or anything can eat the slop they serve here."

"But—"

"That was just to get you away from those two," the gargoyle shrugged. "You see, I'm shy."

"Shy about what?"

"About asking you for a job, of course!"

I decided I would definitely have to keep my voice down in the future. My quiet conversation with Brockhurst seemed to have attracted the attention of half the Bazaar.

"Look . . . um . . ."

"Gus!" the gargoyle supplied.

"Yes, well, ah, Gus, I'm really not hiring—"

"I know. Your partner is," Gus interrupted. "But you're here and he isn't, so I figured I'd make our pitch to you before the second team roster is completely filled."

"Oh!" I said, not knowing what else to say.

"The way I see it," the gargoyle continued, "we could do you a lot of good. You're a Klahd, aren't you?"

"I'm from Klah," I acknowledged stiffly.

"Well, if my memory serves me correctly, warfare in that dimension isn't too far advanced technologically."

"We have crossbows and catapults," I informed him. "At least the other side does."

"That's what I said," Gus agreed. "Primitive. To stop that force, all you need is air support and a little firepower. We can supply both, and we'll work cheap, both of us for one gold piece."

Now I was sure I had underestimated the market value of gold pieces. Still, the price was tempting.

"I dunno, Gus," I said cagily. "Ajax there is supposed to be a pretty good Archer."

"Archers," the gargoyle snorted. "I'm talking about *real* firepower. The kind my partner can give you."

"Who *is* your partner?" I asked. "He isn't short and blue by any chance, is he?"

"Naw," Gus replied, pointing to the far corner. "That's the Gremlin. He came in with the Archer."

"A Gremlin?" I said, following his finger.

Sure enough, perched on a chair in the corner was a small, elfish character. Mischievous eyes danced in his soft blue face as he nodded to me in silent recognition. Reflexively, I smiled and nodded back. Apparently I owed Ajax an apology.

"I thought Gremlins didn't exist," I commented casually to Gus.

"A lot of folks think that," the gargoyle agreed. "But you can see for yourself, they're real."

I wasn't sure. In the split second I had taken my eyes off the Gremlin to speak with Gus, he had vanished without a trace. I was tempted to go looking for him, but Gus was talking again.

"Just a second and I'll introduce you to my partner," he was saying. "He's here somewhere."

As he spoke, the gargoyle began rummaging about his own body, feeling his armpits and peering into the wrinkles on his skin.

I watched curiously, until my attention was arrested by a small lizard that had crawled out of one of the gargoyle's wing folds and was now regarding me fixedly from Gus's right shoulder. It was only about three inches long, but glowed with a brilliant orange hue. There were blotchy red patterns which seemed to crawl about the lizard's skin with a life of their own. The overall effect was startlingly beautiful.

"Is that your lizard?" I asked.

"There he is!" Gus crowed triumphantly, snatching the reptile from his shoulder and cupping it in his hands. "Meet Berfert. He's the partner I was telling you about."

"Hello, Berfert," I smiled, extending a finger to stroke him.

The gargoyle reacted violently, jerking the lizard back out of my reach.

"Careful, there," he warned. "That's a good way to lose a finger."

"I wasn't going to hurt him," I explained.

"No, he was about to hurt you!" Gus countered. "Berfert's a salamander, a walking firebomb. We get along because I'm one of the few beings around that won't burn to a crisp when I touch him."

"Oh," I said with sudden understanding. "So when you said 'firepower'—"

"I meant *firepower*," Gus finished. "Berfert cleans 'em out on the ground, and I work 'em over from the air. Well, what do you say? Have we got a deal?"

"I'll . . . um . . . have to talk it over with my partner," I countered.

"Fine," Gus beamed. "I'll start packing."

He was gone before I could stop him.

I sagged against the counter, wishing fervently for Aahz's return. As if in answer to my thoughts, my mentor burst through the door, following closely by Tanda.

My greeting died in my throat when I saw his scowl. Aahz was not in a good mood.

"I thought I told you to wait outside," he bellowed at me.

"Calm down, Aahz," Tanda soothed. "I thought he'd be more comfortable waiting in here. Besides, there's no reason to get upset. We're here and he's here. Nothing has gone wrong."

"You haven't been dealing with any Deveels?" Aahz asked suspiciously.

"I haven't even talked with any," I protested.

"Good!" he retorted, slightly mollified. "There's hope for you yet, kid."

"I told you he could stay out of trouble," Tanda smiled triumphantly. "Isn't that right, handsome?"

Try as I might, I couldn't bring myself to answer her.

Chapter Fifteen:

"I'll worry about it tomorrow."
—S. O'HARA

"UM . . . are the mercenaries waiting outside?" I
asked finally.

"You didn't answer her question, kid," Aahz
observed, peering at me with renewed suspicion.

"Don't strain your neck looking for your troops,
handsome," Tanda advised me. "There weren't any.
It seems our mighty negotiator has met his match."

"Those bandits!" Aahz exploded. "Do you have
any idea what it would cost us if I had agreed to pay
their bar bill as part of the contract? If that's a non-
profit group, I want to audit their books."

My hopes for salvation sank like a rock.

"You didn't hire them?" I asked.

"No, I didn't," Aahz scowled. "And that moves
us back to square one. Now we've got to recruit a
force one at a time."

"Did you try—" I began.

"Look, kid," Aahz interrupted with a snarl, "I

did the best I could, and I got nowhere. I'd like to see you do better."

"He already has!" Brockhurst announced, rising from his seat. "While you were wasting time, Skeeve here has hired himself a fighting team."

"He what?" Aahz bellowed, turning on his critic. "Brockhurst! What are you doing here?"

"Waiting for orders in our upcoming campaign," the Imp replied innocently.

"What campaign?" Aahz glowered.

"The one on Klah, of course," Brockhurst blinked. "Haven't you told him yet, boss?"

"Boss?" Aahz roared. "Boss?"

"No need ta shout," Ajax grumbled, turning to face the assemblage. "We hear ya plain enough."

"Ajax!" Tanda exclaimed gleefully.

"Tanda!" the old man yelped back.

She was at him in a bound, but he smoothly interposed his bow between them.

"Easy, girl," he laughed. "None of your athletic greetings. I'm not as young as I used to be, ya know."

"You old fraud!" Tanda teased. "You'll outlive us all."

Ajax shrugged dramatically. "That kinda depends on how good a general the youngster there is," he commented.

"Kid," Aahz growled through gritted teeth, "I want to talk to you! *Now!*"

"I know that temper!" Gus announced, emerging from the back room.

"Gus!" Aahz exclaimed.

"In the stone!" the gargoyle confirmed. "Are you in on this expedition? The boss didn't say anything about working with Perverts."

Instead of replying, Aahz sank heavily into a chair and hid his face in his hands.

"Tanda!" he moaned. "Tell me again about how this kid can stay out of trouble."

"Um . . . Aahz," I said cautiously, "could I talk to you for a minute . . . privately?"

"Why, I think that's an excellent idea . . . boss," he said.

The smile he gave me wasn't pleasant.

"Kid!" Aahz moaned after I had finished my tale. "How many times do I have to tell you? This is the Bazaar at Deva! You've *got* to be careful what you say and to whom, especially when there's money involved."

"But I told them nothing was definite until we found out if you had hired someone else," I protested.

"But I didn't hire anyone else, so now the deal is final," Aahz sighed.

"Can't we get out of it?" I asked hopefully.

"Back out of a deal on Deva?" Aahz shook his head. "That would get us barred from the Bazaar so fast it would make your head spin. Remember, the Merchants Association runs this dimension."

"Well, you said you wanted outside help," I pointed out.

"I didn't expect to go that far outside," he grimaced. "An Imp, a senile Archer, and a gargoyle."

"And a salamander," I added.

"Gus is still bumming around with Berfert?" Aahz asked, brightening slightly. "That's a plus."

"The only really uncertain factor," I said thoughtfully, "is the Gremlin."

"How do you figure that?" Aahz yawned.

"Well, he's been following Ajax. The question is, why? And will he follow us to Klah?"

"Kid," Aahz said solemnly, "I've told you before. There are no such things as Gremlins."

"But Aahz, I saw him."

"Don't let it bother you, kid," Aahz sympathized. "After a day like you've been through, I wouldn't be surprised if you saw a Jabberwocky."

"What's a—"

"Is everything set?" Tanda asked, joining our conversation.

"About as set as we'll ever be," Aahz sighed. "Though if you want my honest opinion, with a crew like this, we're set more for a zoo than a war."

"Aahz is a bit critical of my choice in recruits," I confided.

"What's your gripe, Aahz?" she asked, cocking her head. "I thought you and Gus were old foxhole buddies."

"I'm not worried about Gus," Aahz put in hastily. "Or Berfert either. That little lizard's terrific under fire."

"Well, I can vouch for Ajax," Tanda informed him. "Don't let his age fool you. I'd rather have him backing my move than a whole company of counterfeit archers."

"Is he really from Archiah?" Aahz asked skeptically.

"That's what he's said as long as I've known him," Tanda shrugged. "And after seeing him shoot, I've got no reason to doubt it. Why?"

"I've never met a genuine Archer before," Aahz said. "For a while I was willing to believe the whole dimension was a legend. Well, if he can shoot half as well as Archers are supposed to, I've got no gripes having him on the team.''

I started to feel a little better. Unfortunately, Aahz noticed my smile.

"The Imp is another story," he said grimly. "I'm not wild about working with any Imp, but to hire one without powers is a waste of good money.''

"Don't forget he's an Assassin," Tanda pointed out. "Powers or no powers, I'll bet we find a use for him. When we were talking with the Gremlin just now—"

"Now don't *you* start on that!" Aahz snarled.

"Start on what?" Tanda blinked.

"The Gremlin bit," Aahz scowled. "Any half-wit knows there are no such things as Gremlins."

"Do you want to tell him that?" Tanda smiled. "I'll call him over here and . . . oh, rats! He's gone again.''

"If you're quite through," Aahz grumbled, rising from his chair, "we'd best get moving. There's a war waiting for us, you know.''

"Oops! That reminds me!" Tanda exclaimed, fishing inside her tunic.

"I know I shouldn't ask," Aahz signed, "but what—"

"Here!" Tanda announced, flipping him a familiar object.

It was a metal rod about eight inches long and two inches in diameter with a button on one end of it.

"A D-Hopper!" I cried, recognizing the device instantly.

"It's the same one you gave Isstvan," Tanda smiled proudly. "I lifted it from him when we parted company. You'll probably want to undo whatever you did to the controls before you use it, though."

"If I can remember for sure," Aahz scowled, staring at the device.

"I thought it might come in handy in case we get separated on this job and you need a fast exit," Tanda shrugged.

"The thought's appreciated," Aahz smiled, putting an arm around her.

"Does this mean you'll be able to teach me how to travel the dimensions?" I asked hopefully.

"Not now I won't," Aahz grimaced. "We've got a war to fight, remember?"

"Oh! Yes, of course."

"Well, get your troops together and let's go," Aahz ordered.

"Okay," I agreed, rising from my chair. "I'll get Gleep and . . . wait a minute! Did you say *my* troops?"

"You hired 'em, you lead 'em," my mentor smiled.

"But you're—"

"I'll be your military advisor, of course," Aahz continued casually. "But the job of Fearless Leader is all yours. You're the court magician, remember?"

I swallowed hard. Somehow this had never entered into my thinking.

"But what do I do?" I asked desperately.

"Well," Aahz drawled. "First, I'd advise you to move 'em outside so we can all head for Klah together . . . that is, unless you're willing to leave your dragon behind."

That didn't even deserve an answer. I turned to face the troops, sweeping them with what I hoped was a masterful gaze which would immediately command their attention.

No one noticed. They were all involved in a jovial conversation.

I cleared my throat noisily.

Nothing.

I considered going over to their table.

"Listen up!" Aahz barked suddenly, scaring me half to death.

The conversation stopped abruptly and all heads swiveled my way.

"Aah . . ." I began confidently. "We're ready to go now. Everybody outside. Wait for me by the dragon."

"Right, boss!" Brockhurst called, starting for the door.

"I'll be a minute, youngster," Ajax wheezed, struggling to rise.

"Here, Gramps," Gus said. "Let me give you a hand."

"Name's not Gramps, it's Ajax!" the Archer scowled.

"Just trying to be helpful," the gargoyle apologized.

"I kin' stand up by myself," Ajax insisted. "Just 'cause I'm old don't mean I'm helpless."

I glanced to Aahz for help, but he and Tanda were already headed out.

As I turned back to Ajax, I thought I caught a glimpse of a small, blue figure slipping out through the door ahead of us. If it was the Gremlin, he was nowhere in sight when I finally reached the street.

Chapter Sixteen:

"Myth-conceptions are the major cause of wars!"

—A. HITLER

FORTUNATELY, the army had not moved from the position it held when we left for Deva. I say fortunately because Aahz pointed out they might well have renewed their advance in our absence. If that had happened, we would have returned to find ourselves behind the enemy lines, if not actually in the middle of one of their encampments.

Of course, he pointed this out to me after we had arrived back on Klah. Aahz is full of helpful little tidbits of information, but his timing leaves a lot to be desired.

Ajax lost no time upon our arrival. Moving with a briskness that belied his years, he strung his bow and stood squinting at the distant encampments.

"Well, youngster," he asked, never taking his eyes from the enemy's formations, "what's my first batch of targets?"

120

His eagerness took me aback a bit, but Aahz covered for me neatly.

"First," he said loftily, "we'll have to hold a final planning session."

"We didn't expect to have you along, Ajax," Tanda added. "Having a genuine Archer on our side naturally calls for some drastic revisions of our battle plans."

"Don't bother me none," Ajax shrugged. "Just wanted ta let you know I was ready to earn my keep. Take yer time. Seen too many wars messed up 'cause nobody bothered to do any plannin'! If ya don't mind, though, think I'll take me a little nap. Jes' holler when ya want some shootin' done."

"Ah . . . go ahead, Ajax," I agreed.

Without further conversation, Ajax plopped down and pulled his cloak a bit closer about him. Within a few minutes, he was snoring lightly, but I noticed his bow was still in his grip.

"Now there's a seasoned soldier," Aahz observed. "Gets his sleep when and where he can."

"You want me to do a little scouting, boss?" Gus asked.

"Um . . ." I hesitated, glancing quickly at Aahz.

Aahz caught my look and gave a small nod.

"Sure, Gus," I finished. "We'll wait for you here."

"I'll scout in the other direction," Brockhurst volunteered.

"Okay," I nodded. "Aahz, can you give 'em a quick briefing?"

I was trying to drop the load in Aahz's lap, but he joined the conversation as smoothly as if we had rehearsed it this way.

"There are a couple of things we need specific information on," he said solemnly. "First, we need a battlefield, small with scattered cover. Gus, you check that out. You know what we're going to need. Brockhurst, see what details you can bring back on the three nearest encampments."

Both scouts nodded briskly.

"And both of you, stay out of sight," Aahz warned. "The information's no good to us if you don't come back."

"C'mon, Aahz," Gus admonished. "What have they got that can put a dent in the old rock?"

He demonstrated by smashing his forearm into a sapling. The tree went down, apparently without affecting the gargoyle's arm in the slightest.

"I don't know," Aahz admitted. "And I don't want to know, yet. You're one of our surprise weapons. No point in giving the enemy an advance warning. Get my meaning?"

"Got it, Aahz," Gus nodded, and lumbered off.

"Be back in a bit," Brockhurst said with a wave of his hand, heading off in the opposite direction.

"Now that we've got a minute," I murmured to Aahz as I returned Brockhurst's wave, "would you mind telling me what our final plan is? I don't even know what the preliminary plans were."

"That's easy," Aahz replied. "We don't have one . . . yet."

"Well, when are we going to form one?" I asked with forced patience.

"Probably on the battlefield," Aahz yawned. "Until then it's pointless. There're too many variables until then."

"Wouldn't it be a good idea to have at least a

general idea as to what we're going to do *before* we wander out on the battlefield?" I insisted. "It would do a lot for my peace of mind."

"Oh, I've already got a general idea as to what we'll be doing," Aahz admitted.

"Isn't he sweet?" Tanda grimaced. "Would you mind sharing it with us, Aahz? We've got a stake in this, too."

"Well," he began lazily, "the name of the game is delay and demoralize. The way I figure it, we aren't going to overpower them. We haven't got enough going for us to even try that."

I bit back a sarcastic observation and let him continue.

"Delay and demoralize we should be able to do, though," Aahz smiled. "Right off the bat, we've got two big weapons going for us in that kind of a fight."

"Ajax and Gus," I supplied helpfully.

"Fear and bureaucracy," Aahz corrected.

"How's that again?" Tanda frowned.

"Tanda, my girl," Aahz smiled, "you've been spoiled by your skylarking through the dimensions. You've forgotten how the man on the street thinks. The average person in any dimension doesn't know the first thing about magik, particularly about its limitations. If the kid here tells 'em he can make the sun stop or trees grow upside down, they'll believe him. Particularly if he's got a few strange characters parading around as proof of his power, and I think you'll have to admit, the crew he's got backing him this time around is pretty strange."

"What's bureaucracy?" I asked, finally getting a word in edgewise.

"Red tape . . . the system," Aahz informed me.

"The organization to get things done that keeps things from getting done. In this case, it's called the chain-of-command. An army the size of the one we're facing has to function like a well-oiled machine or it starts tripping over its own feet. I'm betting if we toss a couple of handfuls of sand into its gears, they'll spend more time fighting each other than chasing us."

This was one of the first times Aahz had actually clarified something he said. I wished he hadn't. I was more confused than I had been before.

"Um . . . how are we going to do all this?" I asked.

"We'll be able to tell better after you've had your first war council," Aahz shrugged.

"Aren't we having it now?"

"I meant with the enemy," Aahz scowled. "Sometime in the near future, you're going to have to sit down with one of their officers and decide how this war's going to be fought."

"Me?" I blinked.

"You *are* the leader of the defenses, remember?" Aahz grinned at me.

"It's part of the job, handsome," Tanda confirmed.

"Wait a minute," I interrupted. "It just came to me. I think I have a better idea."

"This I've got to hear," Aahz grinned.

"Shut up, Aahz," Tanda ordered, poking him in the ribs. "Whatcha got, handsome?"

"We've got a couple of trained Assassins on our side, don't we?" I observed. "Why don't we just put 'em to work? If enough officers suddenly turn up dead, odds are the army will fall apart. Right?"

"It won't work, kid," Aahz announced bluntly.

"Why not?"

"We can bend the rules, but we can't break 'em," Aahz explained. "Wars are fought between the troops. Killing off the officers without engaging their troops goes against tradition. I doubt if your own force would stand still for it. Old troopers like Ajax would have no part of a scheme like that."

"He's right," Tanda confirmed. "Assassins take contracts on individuals in personal feuds, but not against the general staff of an army."

"But it would be so easy," I insisted.

"Look at it this way, kid," Aahz put in. "If you could do it, they could do it. The way things are now, you're exempt from Assassins. Would you really want to change that?"

"What do I say in a war council?" I asked.

"I'll brief you on that when the time comes," Aahz reassured me. "Right now we have other things to plan."

"Such as what?" Tanda asked.

"Such as what to do about those signal towers," Aahz retorted, jerking his head at one of the distant structures.

"We probably won't have time to break their code, so the next best thing is to disrupt their signals somehow. Now, you said you picked up some special effects items back at the Bazaar. Have you got anything we could use on the signal towers?"

"I'm not sure," Tanda frowned thoughtfully. "I wish you had said something about that before I went shopping."

"What about Ajax?" I suggested.

"What about him?" Aahz countered.

"How close would he have to be to the towers to disrupt things with his archery?"

"I don't know," Aahz shrugged. "Why don't you ask him."

Eager to follow up on my own suggestion, I squatted down next to the dozing bowman.

"Um . . . Ajax," I called softly.

"Whatcha need, youngster?" the old man asked, coming instantly awake.

"Do you see those signal towers?" I asked, pointing at the distant structures.

Ajax rose to his feet and squinted in the indicated direction. "Sure can," he nodded.

"We . . . um . . . I was wondering," I explained, "can you use your bow to disrupt their signals?"

In response, Ajax drew an arrow from beneath his cloak, cocked it, and let fly before I could stop him.

The shaft disappeared in the direction of the nearest tower. With sinking heart, I strained my eyes trying to track its flight.

There was a man standing on the tower's platform, his standard leaning against the railing beside him. Suddenly, his standard toppled over, apparently breaking off a handspan from its crosspiece. The man bent and retrieved the bottom portion of the pole, staring with apparent confusion at the broken end.

"Any other targets?" Ajax asked.

He was leaning casually on his bow, his back to the tower. He hadn't even bothered watching to see if his missile struck its mark.

"Um . . . not just now, Ajax," I assured him. "Go back to sleep."

"Fine by me, sonny," Ajax smiled, resettling himself. "There'll be plenty of targets tomorrow."

"How do you figure that?" I asked.

"According to that signal I just cut down," he grinned, "the army's fixin' to move out tomorrow."

"You can read the signals?" I blinked.

"Sure," Ajax nodded. "There're only about eight different codes armies use, and I know 'em all. It's part of my trade."

"And they're moving out tomorrow?" I pressed.

"That's what I said." The bowman scowled. "What's the matter, are you deaf?"

"No," I assured him hastily. "It just changes our plans is all. Go back to sleep."

Returning to our little conference, I found Aahz and Tanda engrossed in a conversation with Brockhurst.

"Bad news, kid," Aahz informed me. "Brockhurst here says the army's going to move out tomorrow."

"I know," I said. "I just found out from Ajax. Can you read the signal flags too, Brockhurst?"

"Naw," the Imp admitted. "But the Gremlin can."

"What Gremlin?" Aahz bared his teeth.

"He was here a minute ago," Brockhurst scowled, looking around.

"Well, handsome," Tanda sighed, eyeing me, "I think we just ran out of planning time. Better call your dragon. I think we're going to need all the help we can get tomorrow."

Gleep had wandered off shortly after our arrival, though we could still hear him occasionally as he poked about in the underbrush.

"You go get the dragon, Tanda," Aahz ordered.

"Though it escapes me how he's supposed to be any help. The 'boss' here and I have to discuss his war council tomorrow."

Any confidence I might have built up listening to Aahz's grand plan earlier fled me. Tanda was right. We had run out of time.

Chapter Seventeen:

"Diplomacy is the delicate weapon of the civilized warrior."

—HUN, A.T.

WE waited patiently for our war council. The two of us, Aahz and me. Against an army.

This was, of course, Aahz's idea. Left to my own devices, I wouldn't be caught dead in this position.

Trying to ignore that unfortunate choice of words, I cleared my throat and spoke to Aahz out of the corner of my mouth.

"Aahz?"

"Yeah, kid?"

"How long are we going to stand here?"

"Until they notice us and do something about it."

Terrific. Either we'd rot where we stood, or someone would shoot us full of arrows.

We were standing about twenty yards from one of the encampments, with nothing between us and them but meadow. We could see clearly the bustle of activity within the encampment and, in theory, there was nothing keeping them from seeing us. This is why we were standing where we were, to draw attention to ourselves. Unfortunately, so far no one had noticed.

It had been decided that Aahz and I would work alone on this first sortie to hide the true strength of our force. It occurred to me that it also hid the true weakness of our force, but I felt it would be tactless to point this out.

At first, Brockhurst had argued in favor of his coming along with me instead of Aahz, claiming that as an Imp he had much more experience at bargaining than a demon. It was pointed out to him rather forcefully by Aahz that in this instance we weren't bargaining for glass beads or whoopie cushions, but for a war . . . and if the Imp wanted to prove to Aahz that he knew more about fighting. . . .

Needless to say, Brockhurst backed down at that point. This was good, as it saved me from having to openly reject his offer. I mean, I may not be the fastest learner around, but I could still distinctly remember Aahz getting the best of Brockhurst the last time the two of them had squared off for a bargaining session.

Besides, if this meeting went awry, I wanted my mentor close at hand to share the consequences with me.

So here we stood, blatantly exposed to the enemy without even a sword for our defense. That was another of Aahz's brainstorms. He argued that our being unarmed accomplished three things. First, it showed that we were here to talk, not to fight. Second, it demonstrated our faith in my magical abilities to defend us. Third, it encouraged our enemy to meet us similarly unarmed.

He also pointed out that Ajax would be hiding in

the tree line behind us with strung bow and cocked arrow, and would probably be better at defending us if anything went wrong than a couple of swords would.

He was right, of course, but it did nothing to settle my nerves as we waited.

"Heads up, kid," Aahz murmured. "We've got company."

Sure enough, a rather stocky individual was striding briskly across the meadow in our direction.

"Kid!" Aahz hissed suddenly. "Your disguise!"

"What about it?" I whispered back.

"It isn't!" came the reply.

He was right! I had carefully restored his "dubious character" appearance, but had forgotten completely about changing my own. Having our motley crew accept my leadership in my normal form had caused me to overlook the fact that Klahds are harder to impress than demons.

"Should I—" I began.

"Too late!" Aahz growled. "Fake it."

The soldier was almost upon us now, close enough for me to notice when he abandoned his bored expression and forced a smile.

"I'm sorry, folks," he called with practiced authority. "You'll have to clear the area. We'll be moving soon and you're blocking the path."

"Call your duty officer!" Aahz boomed back at him.

"My who?" the soldier scowled.

"Duty officer, officer of the day, commander, whatever you call whoever's currently in charge of your formation," Aahz clarified. "Somebody's got to be running things, and if you're officer material, I'm the Queen of the May."

Whether or not the soldier understood Aahz's allusion (I didn't), he caught the general implication.

"Yeah, there's someone in charge," he snarled, his complexion darkening slightly. "He's a very busy man right now, too busy to stand around talking to civilians. We're getting ready to move our troops, mister, so take your son and get out of the way. If you want to watch the soldiers, you'll have to follow along and watch us when we camp tonight."

"Do you have any idea who you're talking to?" I said in a surprisingly soft voice.

"I don't care who your father is, sonny," the soldier retorted. "We're trying to—"

"The name's not 'sonny,' it's *Skeeve!*" I hissed, drawing myself up. "Court magician to the kingdom of Possiltum, pledged to that kingdom's defense. Now I advise you to call your officer . . . or do you want to wake up tomorrow morning on a lily pad?"

The soldier recoiled a step and stood regarding me suspiciously.

"Is he for real?" he asked Aahz skeptically.

"How's your taste for flies?" Aahz smiled.

"You mean he can really—"

"Look," interrupted Aahz, "I'm not playing servant to the kid because of his terrific personality, if you know what I mean."

"I see . . . um. . . ." The soldier was cautiously backing toward the encampment. "I'll . . . um . . . I'll bring my commanding officer."

"We'll be here," Aahz assured him.

The soldier nodded and retreated with noticeably greater speed than he had displayed approaching us.

"So far, so good," my mentor said with a grin.

"What's wrong with my personality?" I asked bluntly.

Aahz sighed. "Later, kid. For the time being, concentrate on looking aloof and dignified, okay?"

Okay or not, there wasn't much else to do while we waited for the officer to put in his appearance.

Apparently, news of our presence spread through the encampment in record time, for a crowd of soldiers gathered at the edge of the camp long before we saw any sign of the officer. It seemed all preparations to move were suspended at least temporarily while the soldiers lined up and craned their necks to gawk at us.

It was kind of a nice feeling to have caused such a sensation, until I noticed several soldiers were taking time to strap on weapons and armor before joining the crowd.

"Aahz!" I whispered.

"Yeah, kid?"

"I thought this was supposed to be a peaceful meeting."

"It is," he assured me.

"But they're arming!" I pointed out.

"Relax, kid," he whispered back. "Remember, Ajax is covering us."

I tried to focus on that thought. Then I saw what was apparently the officer approaching us flanked by two soldiers, and I focused on the swords they were all wearing.

"Aahz!" I hissed.

"Relax, kid," Aahz advised me. "Remember Ajax."

I remembered. I also remembered we were vastly outnumbered.

"I understand you gentlemen are emissaries of Possiltum?" the officer asked, coming to a halt in front of us.

I nodded stiffly, hoping the abruptness of my motion would be interpreted as annoyance rather than fear.

"Fine," the officer smirked. "Then as the first representative of the Empire to contact a representative of Possiltum, I have the pleasure of formally declaring war on your kingdom."

"What is your name?" Aahz asked casually.

"Claude," the officer responded. "Why do you ask?"

"The historians like details," Aahz shrugged. "Well, Claude, as the first representative of Possiltum to meet with a representative of your Empire in times of war, it is our pleasure to demand your unconditional surrender."

That got a smile out of the officer.

"Surrender?" he chortled. "To a cripple and a child? You must be mad. Even if I had the authority to do such a thing, I wouldn't."

"That's right." Aahz shook his head in mock self-admonishment. "We should have realized. Someone in charge of a supply company wouldn't swing much weight in an army like this, would he?"

We had chosen this particular group of soldiers to approach specifically because they were a supply unit. That meant they were lightly armed and hopefully not an elite fighting group.

Aahz's barb struck home, however. The officer stopped smiling and dropped his hand to his sword hilt. I found myself thinking again of Ajax's protection.

"I have more than enough authority to deal with you two," he hissed.

"Authority, maybe," I yawned. "But I frankly doubt you have the power to stand against us."

As I mentioned, I did not feel as confident as I sounded. The officer's honor guard had mimicked his action, so that now all three of our adversaries were standing ready to draw their swords.

"Very well," Claude snarled. "You've been warned. Now we're going to bring our wagons across this spot, and if you're on it when we get here you've no one to blame but yourselves."

"Accepted!" Aahz leered. "Shall we say noon tomorrow?"

"Tomorrow?" the officer scowled. "What's wrong with right now?"

"Come, come, Claude," Aahz admonished. "We're talking about the first engagement of a new campaign. Surely you want some time to plan your tactics."

"Tactics?" Claude echoed thoughtfully.

". . . and to pass the word to your superiors that you're leading the opening gambit," Aahz continued casually.

"Hmm," the officer murmured.

". . . and to summon reinforcements," I supplied. "Unless, of course, you want to keep all the glory for yourself."

"Glory!"

That did it. Claude pounced on the word like a Deveel on a gold piece. Aahz had been right in assuming supply officers don't see combat often.

"I . . . uh . . . I don't believe we'll require reinforcements," he murmured cagily.

"Are you sure?" Aahz sneered. "The odds are only about a hundred to one in your favor."

"But he *is* a magician," Claude smiled. "A good officer can't be too careful. Still, it would be pointless to involve too many officers . . . er . . . I mean, soldiers in a minor skirmish.''

"Claude," Aahz said with grudging admiration, "I can see yours is a military mind without equal. Win or lose, I look forward to having you as an opponent.''

"And you, sir," the officer returned with equal formality. "Shall we say noon then?''

"We'll be here," Aahz nodded.

With that, the officer turned and strode briskly back to his encampment, his bodyguard trudging dutifully beside him.

Our comrades were bristling with questions when we reentered the tree line.

"Is it set, boss?" Brockhurst asked.

"Any trouble?" Tanda pressed.

"Piece of cake," Aahz bragged. "Right, kid?''

"Well," I began modestly, "I was a little worried when they started to reach for their swords. I would have been terrified if I didn't know Ajax was . . . say, where is Ajax?''

"He's up in that clump of bushes," Gus informed me, jerking a massive thumb at a thicket of greenery on the edge of the tree line. "He should be back by now.''

When we found Ajax, he was fast asleep curled around his bow. We had to shake him several times to wake him.

Chapter Eighteen:

"Just before the battle, Mother, I was thinking most of you . . ."
—SONNY BARKER

A LONG, slimy tongue assaulted me from the darkness, accompanied by a blast of bad breath which could have only one source.

"Gleep!"

I started to automatically cuff the dragon away, then had a sudden change of heart.

"Hi, fella," I smiled, scratching his ear. "Lonely?"

In response, my pet flopped on his side with a thud that shook the ground. His serpentine neck was long enough that he managed to perform this maneuver without moving his head from my grasp.

His loyal affection brought a smile to my face for the first time since I had taken up my lonely vigil. It was a welcome antidote to my nervous insomnia.

I was leaning against a tree, watching the pinpoints of light that marked the enemy's encampment. Even though the day's events had left me exhausted, I found myself unable to sleep, my mind awash with fears and anticipation of tomorrow's clash. Not wishing to draw attention to my discomfort, I had crept to this place to be alone.

As stealthy as I had attempted to be, however, apparently Gleep had noted my movement and come to keep me company.

"Oh, Gleep," I whispered. "What are we going to do?"

For his answer, he snuggled closer against me and laid his head in my lap for additional patting. He seemed to have unshakable faith in my ability to handle any crisis as it arose. I wished with all my heart I shared his confidence.

"Skeeve?" came a soft voice from my right.

I turned my head and found Tanda standing close beside me. The disquieting thing about having an Assassin for a friend is that they move so silently.

"Can I talk to you for a moment?"

"Sure, Tanda," I said, patting the ground next to me. "Have a seat."

Instead of sitting at the indicated spot, she sank to the ground where she stood and curled her legs up under her.

"It's about Ajax," she began hesitantly. "I hate to bother you, but I'm worried about him."

"What's wrong?" I asked.

"Well, the team's been riding him about falling asleep today when he was supposed to be covering you," she explained. "He's taking it pretty hard."

"I wasn't too wild about it myself," I commented bitterly. "It's a bad feeling to realize that we really were alone out there. If anything *had* gone wrong, we would have been cut to shreds while placidly waiting for our expert bowman to intercede!"

"I know." Tanda's voice was almost too soft to be heard. "And I don't blame you for feeling like that. In a way, I blame myself."

"Yourself?" I blinked. "Why?"

"I vouched for him, Skeeve," she whispered. "Don't you remember?"

"Well, sure," I admitted. "But you couldn't have known—"

"But I should have," she interrupted bitterly. "I should have realized how old he is now. He shouldn't be here, Skeeve. That's why I wanted to talk to you about doing something."

"Me?" I asked, genuinely startled. "What do you want me to do?"

"Send him back," Tanda urged. "It isn't fair to you to endanger your mission because of him, and it isn't fair to Ajax to put him in a spot like this."

"That isn't what I meant," I murmured, shaking my head. "I meant why are you talking to me? Aahz is the one you have to convince."

"That's where you're wrong, Skeeve," she corrected. "Aahz isn't leading this group, you are."

"Because of what he said back on Deva?" I smiled. "C'mon, Tanda. You know Aahz. He was just a little miffed. You noticed he's called all the shots so far."

The moonlight glistened in Tanda's hair as she shook her head.

"I do know Aahz, Skeeve. Better than you do," she said. "He's a stickler for chain of command. If he says you're the leader, you're the leader."

"But—"

"Besides," she continued over my protest, "Aahz is only one member of the team. What's important is all the others are counting on you, too. On you, not on Aahz. You hired 'em, and as far as they're concerned, you're the boss.''

The frightening thing was she was right. I hadn't really stopped to think about it, but everything she said was true. I had just been too busy with my own worries to reflect on it. Now that I realized the full extent of my responsibilities, a new wave of doubts assaulted me. I wasn't even that sure of myself as a magician, and as a leader of men. . . .

"I'll have to think about it," I stalled.

"You don't have much time," she pointed out. "You've got a war scheduled to start tomorrow."

There was a crackling in the brush to our left, interrupting our conversation.

"Boss?" came Brockhurst's soft hail. "Are you busy?"

"Sort of," I called back.

"Well, this will only take a minute."

Before I could reply, two shadows detached themselves from the brush and drew closer. One was Brockhurst, the other was Gus. I should have known from the noise that the gargoyle was accompanying Brockhurst. Like Tanda, the Imp could move like a ghost.

"We were just talking about Ajax," Brockhurst informed me, squatting down to join our conference.

The gargoyle followed suit.

"Yeah," Gus confirmed. "The three of us wanted to make a suggestion to you."

"Right," Brockhurst nodded. "Gus and me and the Gremlin."

"The Gremlin?" I asked.

The Imp craned his neck to peer around him.

"He must have stayed back at camp," he shrugged.

"About Ajax," Tanda prompted.

"We think you should pull him from the team," Gus announced. "Send him back to Deva and out of the line of fire."

"It's not for us," Brockhurst hastened to clarify. "It's for him. He's a nice old guy, and we'd hate to see anything happen to him."

"He is pretty old," I murmured.

"Old!" Gus exclaimed. "Boss, the Gremlin says he's tailed him for over two hundred years . . . two hundred! According to him, Ajax was old when their paths first crossed. It won't kill him to miss this one war, but it might kill him to fight in it."

"Why is the Gremlin tailing him, anyway?" I asked.

"I've told you before, kid," a voice boomed in my ear, "gremlins don't exist."

With that pronouncement, Aahz sank down at my side, between me and Tanda. As I attempted to restore my heartbeat to normal, it occurred to me I knew an awful lot of light-footed people.

"Hi, Aahz," I said, forcing a smile. "We were just talking about—"

"I know, I heard," Aahz interrupted. "And for a change I agree."

"You do?" I blinked.

"Sure," he yawned. "It's a clear-cut breach of contract. He hired out his services as a bowman, and the first assignment you give him, he literally lies down on the job."

Actually, it had been the second assignment. I had a sudden flash recollection of Ajax drawing and firing in a smooth, fluid motion, cutting down a signal standard so distant it was barely visible.

"My advice would be to send him back," Aahz

was saying. "If you want to soothe your conscience, give him partial payment and a good recommendation, but the way he is, he's no good to anybody."

Perhaps it was because of Tanda's lecture, but I was suddenly aware that Aahz had specifically stated his suggestion as "advice," not an order.

"Heads up, boss," Brockhurst murmured. "We've got company."

Following his gaze, I saw Ajax stumbling toward us, his ghostlike paleness flickering in the darkness like . . . well, like a ghost. It occurred to me that what had started out as a moment of solitude was becoming awfully crowded.

"Evenin', youngster," he saluted. "Didn't mean to interrupt nothin! Didn't know you folks was havin' a meetin'."

"We . . . ah . . . we were just talking," I explained, suddenly embarrassed.

"I kin guess about what, too," Ajax sighed. "Well, I was goin' to do this private-like, but I suppose the rest o' you might as well hear it, too."

"Do what, Ajax?" I asked.

"Resign," he said. "Seems to me to be the only decent thing to do after what happened today."

"It could have happened to anyone," I shrugged.

"Nice of you to say so, youngster," Ajax smiled; "but I kin see the handwriting on the wall. I'm just too old to be any good to anybody anymore. 'Bout time I admitted it to myself."

I found myself noticing the droop in his shoulders and a listlessness that hadn't been there when we first met on Deva.

"Don't fret about payin' me," Ajax continued. "I didn't do nothin', so I figger you don't owe me nothin'. If somebody'll just blip me back to Deva, I'll get outta your way and let you fight your war the way it should be fought."

"Well, Ajax," Aahz sighed, rising to his feet and extending his hand. "We're going to miss you."

"Just a minute!" I found myself saying in a cold voice. "Are you trying to tell me you're breaking our contract?"

Ajax's head came up with a snap.

"I expected better from a genuine Archer," I concluded.

"I wouldn't call it a breach of contract, youngster," the old bowman corrected me carefully. "More like a termination by mutual consent. I'm jes' too old—"

"Old?" I interrupted. "I knew you were old when I hired you. I knew you were old when I planned my strategy for tomorrow's fight around that bow of yours. I knew you were old, Ajax, but I didn't know you were a coward!"

There was a sharp intake of breath somewhere nearby, but I didn't see who it was. My attention was focused on Ajax. It was no longer a defeated, drooping old man, but a proud, angry warrior who loomed suddenly over me.

"Sonny," he growled, "I know I'm old, 'cause in my younger days I would have killed you for sayin' that. I never ran from a fight in my life, and I never broke a contract. If you got some shootin' fer me to do tomorrow, I'll do it. Then maybe you'll see what havin' a genuine Archer on your side is all about!"

With that, he spun on his heel and stalked off into the darkness.

It had been a calculated risk, but I still found I was

covered with cold sweat from facing the old man's
anger. I also realized the rest of the group was staring
at me in silent expectation.

"I suppose you're all wondering why I did that," I
said, smiling.

I had hoped for a response, but the silence continued.

"I appreciate all your advice, and hope you continue to give it in the future. But I'm leading this
force, and the final decisions have to be mine."

Out of the corner of my eye, I saw Aahz cock his
eyebrow, but I ignored him.

"Everyone, including Ajax, said if I let him go, if I
sent him back to Deva, there would be no harm done.
I disagree. It would have taken away the one thing
the years have left untouched . . . his pride. It would
have confirmed to him his worst fears, that he's
become a useless old man."

I scanned my audience. Not one of them could
meet my eye.

"So he might get killed. So what? He's accepted
that risk in every war he's fought in. I'd rather order
him into a fight knowing for certain he'd be killed
than condemn him to a living death as a washed-up
has-been. This way, he has a chance, and as his
employer, I feel I owe him that chance."

I paused for breath. They were looking at me
again, hanging on my next words.

"One more thing," I snarled. "I don't want to
hear any more talk about him being useless. That old
man still handles a bow better than anyone I've ever
seen. If I can't find a way to use him effectively, then
it's my fault as a tactician, not his! I've got my short-
comings, but I'm not going to blame them on Ajax
any more than I'd blame them on any of you."

Silence reigned again, but I didn't care. I had spoken my piece, and felt no compulsion to blather on aimlessly just to fill the void.

"Well, boss"—Brockhurst cleared his throat getting to his feet—"I think I'll turn in now."

"Me, too," echoed Gus, also rising.

"Just one thing." The Imp paused and met my gaze squarely. "For the record, it's a real pleasure working for you."

The gargoyle nodded his agreement, and the two of them faded into the brush.

There was a soft kiss on my cheek, but by the time I turned my head, Tanda had disappeared.

"You know, kid," Aahz said, "you're going to make a pretty good leader someday."

"Thanks, Aahz," I blinked.

". . . if you live that long," my mentor concluded.

We sat side by side in silence for a while longer. Gleep had apparently dozed off, for he was snoring softly as I continued petting him.

"If it isn't prying," Aahz asked finally, "what is this master plan you have for tomorrow that's built around Ajax?"

I sighed and closed my eyes.

"I haven't got one," I admitted. "I was kind of hoping you'd have a few ideas."

"I was afraid you were going to say that," Aahz grumbled.

Chapter Nineteen:

"What if they gave a war and only one side came—"

—LUCIFER

"WAKE up, kid!"

I returned to consciousness as I was being force-fully propelled sideways along the forest floor, pre-sumably assisted by the ready toe of my mentor.

After I had slid to a stop, I exerted most of my energy and raised my head.

"Aahz," I announced solemnly, "as leader of this team, I have reached another decision. In the future, I want Tanda to wake me up."

"Not a chance," Aahz leered. "She's off scouting our right flank. It's me or the dragon."

Great choice. I suddenly realized how bright it was.

"Hey!" I blinked. "How late is it?"

"Figure we've got about a minute before things start popping," Aahz said casually.

"How long?" I gasped.

Aahz's brow furrowed for a moment as he re-

146

flected on his words. Klahdish units of time still gave him a bit of trouble.

"An hour!" he smiled triumphantly. "That's it. An hour."

"That's better," I sighed, sinking back to a horizontal position.

"On your feet, kid!" Aahz ordered. "We let you sleep as late as we could, but now you're needed to review the troops."

"Have you briefed everybody?" I yawned, sitting up. "Is the plan clear?"

"As clear as it's going to be, all things considered," Aahz shrugged.

"Okay," I responded, rolling to my feet. "Let's go. You can fill me in on any new developments along the way."

Aahz and I had been up most of the night formulating today's plan, and I found I was actually eager to see it implemented.

"You should be thankful you aren't on the other side," Aahz chortled as we moved to join the others. "Old Claude's been making the most of the time we gave him."

"Keeping them busy, is he?" I smiled.

"Since sunup," Aahz confirmed smugly. "Drilling, sharpening swords, never a dull moment in the Empire's army, that's for sure."

I wasn't sure I shared Aahz's enthusiasm for the enemy's spending lots of time sharpening their swords. Fortunately, I was spared the discomfort of replying as Gus lumbered up to us.

"You just missed Brockhurst's report," he informed us. "Still nothing on the left flank."

"Wouldn't we be able to tell from their signals if they were moving up additional support?" I asked.

"If you believe their signals," Aahz countered. "It wouldn't be the first time an army figured out the enemy had broken their code and started sending misleading messages."

"Oh," I said wisely.

"Speaking of signals," Aahz said with a grin, "you know the messages they were sending yesterday? The ones that went 'encountered minor resistance'?"

"I remember," I nodded.

"Well, it seems Claude has decided he needs to up the ante if he's going to get a promotion out of this. Overnight we've become 'armed opposition . . . must be subdued forcefully!' Neat, huh?"

I swallowed hard.

"Does that mean they'll be moving in reinforcements?" I asked, trying to sound casual.

"Not a chance, kid." Aahz winked. "Claude there has turned down every offer of assistance that came down the line. He keeps insisting he can handle it with the company he's commanding."

"I'd say he's got his neck way, way out," Gus commented.

". . . and we're just the ones to chop it off for him," Aahz finished.

"Where's Ajax?" I asked, changing the subject.

"Down at the forest line picking out his firing point," Gus replied. "Don't worry, boss. He's awake."

Actually, that wasn't my worry concerning Ajax at all. In my mind's eye, I could still see his angry stance when I called him a coward the night before.

"Mornin', youngster," the bowman hailed, emerging from the bush. "Think I got us a place all picked out."

"Hi, Ajax," I replied. "Say . . . um . . . when you get a minute, I'd like to talk to you about last night."

"Think nothin' of it," Ajax assured me with a grin. "I've plum fergot about it already."

There was a glint in his eye that contradicted his words, but if he was willing to pretend nothing had happened, I'd go along with it for now.

"I hate to interrupt," Aahz interrupted, "but I think friend Claude's just about ready to make his move."

Sure enough, the distant encampment was lining up in a marching formation. The hand-drawn wagons were packed and aligned, with the escort troops arrayed to the front and sides. The signal tower, despite its appearance, was apparently also portable and was being pushed along at the rear of the formation by several sweating soldiers.

"Late!" Ajax sneered. "I tell ya, youngster, armies are the same in any dimension."

"Okay, kid," Aahz said briskly. "Do your stuff. It's about time we got into position."

I nodded and closed my eyes for concentration. With a few strokes of my mental paintbrush, I altered Gus's features until the gargoyle was the mirror image of myself.

"Pretty good," Ajax commented critically, looking from Gus to me and back again.

I repeated the process, returning Aahz to his "dubious character" disguise.

"Well, we're off," Aahz waved. "Confusion to the enemy!"

Today's plan called for Gus substituting for me. The logic was that should anything go wrong, his stone flesh would not only keep him from harm, but also serve as a shield to defend Aahz.

Somehow it didn't seem right to me, to remain behind in relative safety while sending someone else to take my risks for me. It occurred to me that perhaps I had called the wrong person "coward" last night when speaking with Ajax.

The bowman seemed to accept the arrangement without question, however.

"Follow me, youngster," he cackled. "I don't want to miss any of this!"

With that, he turned and plunged into the brush, leaving me little choice but to trail along behind.

Fortunately, Ajax's chosen vantage point wasn't far. Old or not, I found he set a wicked pace.

Stringing his bow, he crouched and waited, chuckling softly in anticipation.

Settling in beside him, I took a moment to check the energy lines, the invisible streams of energy magicians draw their power from. There were two strong lines nearby, one air, one ground, which was good. While Aahz had taught me how to store the energies internally, with the amount of action scheduled for the day, I wanted all the power I could get.

We could see Aahz and Gus striding with great dignity toward the selected combat point. The opposing force watched them in frozen silence as they took their places.

For a moment, everyone stood in tableau.

Then Claude turned to his force and barked out an order. Immediately a half dozen archers broke from the formation and fanned out on either side of the wagons. Moving with slow deliberation, they each drew and cocked an arrow, then leveled the bows at the two figures blocking the company's progress.

I concentrated my energies.

Claude shouted something at our comrades. They remained motionless.

I concentrated.

The bowmen loosed their missiles. Gus threw up one hand dramatically.

The arrows stopped in mid-air and fell to the ground.

The bowmen looked at each other in amazement. Claude barked another order at them. They shakily drew and fired another barrage.

This one was more ragged than the first, but I managed to stop it as well.

"Nice work, youngster," Ajax exclaimed gleefully. "That's got 'em going."

Sure enough, the neat ranks of soldiers were rippling as the men muttered back and forth among themselves. Claude noted it, too, and ordered his bowmen back into the ranks.

Round one to us!

My elation was short-lived, though. The soldiers were drawing their swords now. The two groups assigned to guarding the sides of the wagon pivoted forward, forming two wings ready to engulf our teammates. As further evidence of Claude's nervousness, he even had the troops assigned to pulling the wagons leave their posts and move up to reinforce the center of his line.

That's what we were waiting for.

"Now, Ajax!" I hissed. "Arch 'em high."

"I remember, youngster," the archer grinned. "I'm ready when you are."

I waited until he raised his bow, then concentrated an intense beam of energy at a point a few inches in front of his bow.

It was like the candle-lighting exercise, and it worked as well now as it had when we had tried it last night.

As each shaft sped from Ajax's bow, it burst into flames and continued on its flight.

Again and again with incredible speed the bowman sent his missiles hissing through my ignition point. It required all my concentration to maintain the necessary stream of energy, moving it occasionally as his point of aim changed.

Finally, he dropped his bow back to his side.

"That oughta do it, youngster," he grinned. "Take a look."

I did. There in the distance, behind the soldiers' lines, thin plumes of smoke were rising from the wagons. In a few moments, Claude's supply company would be without supplies.

If we had a few moments! As we watched, the men began to advance on Aahz and Gus, their swords gleaming in the sun.

"Think we'd better do something about that!" Ajax muttered, raising his bow again.

"Wait a second, Ajax!" I ordered, squinting at the distant figures.

There had been a brief consultation between Aahz and Gus, then the gargoyle stepped back and began gesturing wildly at his companion.

It took me a moment, but I finally got the message. With a smile, I closed my eyes and removed Aahz's disguise.

Pandemonium reigned. The soldiers in the front ranks took one look at the demon opposing them and stampeded for the rear, half trampling the men behind them. As word spread through the formation, it became a rout, though I seriously doubt those in the rear knew what they were running from.

If anyone noticed the burning wagons, they didn't slow once.

"Whooee!" Ajax exclaimed, thumping me on the back. "That did it. Look at 'em run. You'd think those fellers never seed a Pervert before."

"They probably haven't," I commented, trying to massage some feeling back into my shoulder.

"You know," the bowman drawled, squinting at the scene below, "I got me an idea. Them fellers ran off so fast they fergot to signal to anybody. Think we should do it for 'em?"

"How?" I asked.

"Well," he grinned. "I know the signals, and you're a magician. If I told you what signal to run up, could you do it? Without anybody holdin' it?"

"Sure could," I agreed. "What'll we need for the signal?"

"Lemme think," he frowned. "We'll have to get a skull, and a couple of pieces of red cloth, and a black ball, an—"

"Wait a minute, Ajax," I said, holding up a hand. "I think there's an easier signal they'll understand. Watch this."

I sent one more blast of energy out, and the tower platform burst into flames.

"Think they'll get the message?" I smiled.

Ajax stared at the burning tower for a moment.

"Yer pretty good at that, youngster," he murmured finally. "Throwin' fire that far."

"Well," I began modestly, "we magicians can—"

" 'Course," he continued. "If you can do that, then you didn't really need me and Blackie to handle those wagons, did you?"

Too late I realized my mistake.

"Ajax, I—"

"Kinda strange, you goin' to all that trouble jes' to convince me I'm not useless."

"You're not useless," I barked. "Just because sometimes you're not necessary doesn't mean you're useless. I may be young, but I'm old enough to know that."

Ajax regarded me for a moment, then he suddenly smiled.

"Danged if you aren't right, youngst . . . Skeeve," he laughed. "Guess I knew it, but plum fergot it there fer a while. Let's go get some wine from that cask strapped to your dragon. I'd like to thank you proper fer remindin' me."

We headed back to camp together.

Chapter Twenty:

> *"Chain of command is the backbone of military structure and must be strictly obeyed."*
>
> —F. CHRISTIAN

THE mood back at the camp was understandably celebratory. If I had had any hopes for joining in the festivities, however, they were dashed when Aahz hailed me.

"Over here, kid!" he waved. "We've got some planning to do!"

"That's the other side o' bein' a general, youngster," Ajax murmured sympathetically. " 'T'aint all speeches and glory. You go on ahead. I'll do my drinkin' with the boys."

With a jerk of his head, he indicated Gus and Brockhurst who were already at the wine. Tanda was waiting for me with Aahz. That made my choice a little easier.

"Okay, Ajax," I smiled. "I'll catch up with you in a little bit."

"Congratulations, handsome!" Tanda winked as I

joined them. "That was as neat a bit of work as I've seen in a long time."

"Thanks, Tanda," I blushed.

"I see you and Ajax are on speaking terms again," Aahz said, regarding me with cocked eyebrows. "That's not a bad trick in itself. How did you do it?"

"We . . . um . . . we had a long talk," I replied vaguely. "You said we had some planning to do?"

"More like a briefing," Aahz admitted. "Tanda here brought along a few special effects items I think you should know about."

I had completely forgotten about Tanda's errand which had left me alone at the Bazaar. Now that I had been reminded, my curiosity soared.

"Whatcha got, Tanda?" I asked eagerly.

"Nothing spectacular," she shrugged. "Knowing Aahz was involved, I figured we'd be on a tight budget so I stuck to the basics."

"Just show him, huh?" Aahz growled. "Spare us the editorial comments."

She stuck her tongue out at him but produced a small cloth sack from her belt.

"First off," she began, "I thought we could use a little flash powder. It never fails to impress the yokels."

"Flash powder," I said carefully.

"You set fire to it," Aahz supplied. "It burns fast and gives you a cloud of smoke."

"I've got about a dozen small bags of it here," Tanda continued, showing me the contents of her sack. "Various colors and sizes."

"Can I try one?" I asked. "I've never worked with this stuff before."

"Sure," Tanda said. She grinned, extending the

sack. "They're yours to use as you see fit. You might as well know what you've got."

I took the sack and carefully selected one of the small bags from its interior.

"Better toss it to the ground, kid," Aahz cautioned. "Some folks can set it off in their hand, but that takes practice. If you tried it that way now, you'd probably lose a few fingers."

I obediently tossed the bag on the ground a few feet away. Watching it curiously, I focused a quick burst of energy on it.

There was a bright flash of light accompanied by a soft *pop*. Blinking my eyes, I looked at where the bag had been. A small cloud of green smoke hung in the air, slowly dissipating in the breeze.

"That's neat!" I exclaimed, reaching into the sack again.

"Take it easy," Aahz warned. "We don't have that much of the stuff."

"Oh! Right, Aahz," I replied, feeling a little sheepish. "What else do you have, Tanda?"

"Well," she said, smiling, "I guess this would be a pièce-de-résistance."

As she spoke, she seemed to draw something from behind her back. I say "seemed" because I couldn't see anything. From her movements, she looked to be holding a rod about three feet long, but there was nothing in her grasp.

"What is it?" I asked politely.

For a response, she grinned and held whatever it was in front of her. Then she opened her grip and disappeared into thin air.

"Invisibility," Aahz exclaimed. "A cloak of invisibility!"

"Couldn't afford one," came Tanda's voice from somewhere in front of us. "I had to settle for one of these."

What "one of these" was, it turned out, was a sheet of invisibility. It was a sheet of stiff material about three feet by seven feet. Tanda had been carrying it rolled up in a tube, and her disappearance had been caused by the sheet unrolling to its full size.

As she and Aahz chatted excitedly about her new find, I had an opportunity to further my knowledge in the field of invisibility.

Invisible sheets, it seems, were made of roughly the same material as invisible cloaks. Since the sheets were carried, not worn, they did not require the flexibility and softness necessary for a cloak. Consequently, they were considerably cheaper than the cloaks.

The effect was sort of like one-way glass. When you were on the right side of an invisible sheet, you could see through it perfectly well to observe whatever or whoever was on the other side. They, however, could not see you.

We were still discussing the potential uses of the new tool when Brockhurst hastened up to our group.

"Hey, boss!" he called. "We've got company!"

"Who? Where?" I asked calmly.

"Down on the meadow," the Imp responded, pointing. "The Gremlin says there's some kind of group forming out there."

"What Gremlin?" Aahz snarled.

"C'mon, Aahz," Tanda called, starting off. "Let's check this out."

There was indeed a group on the meadow, Empire soldiers all. The puzzling thing was their activity, or specifically their lack of it. They seemed to be simply standing and waiting for something.

"What are they doing, Aahz?" I whispered as we studied the group form the concealment of the tree line.

"They're standing and waiting," Aahz supplied.

"I can see that," I said. "But what are they waiting for?"

"Probably for us," my mentor replied.

"For us?" I blinked. "Why?"

"For a war council," Aahz grinned. "Look at it, kid. Aren't they doing the same thing we did when we wanted to talk? They're even standing in the same spot."

I restudied the group in this light. Aahz was right! The enemy was calling for a war council!

"Do you think we should go out there?" I asked nervously.

"Sure," Aahz replied. "But not right away. Let 'em sweat a little. They kept us waiting the first time, remember?"

It was nearly half an hour before we stepped from the tree line and advanced across the meadow to where the soldiers stood waiting. I had taken the precaution of outfitting Aahz in his "dubious character" disguise for the conference. Myself, I was bearing the invisibility sheet before me, so that though I was walking along beside Aahz, to the soldiers it appeared he was alone.

There were more soldiers at the meeting point than there had been at our first meeting with Claude. Even to my untrained eye, it was apparent that there were more than half a dozen officers present among the honor guard.

"You wish a meeting?" Aahz asked haughtily, drawing to a halt before the group.

There was a ripple of quick consultation among the soldiers. Finally one of them, apparently the leader, stepped forward.

"We wish to speak with your master!" he announced formally.

"He's kinda busy right now," Aahz yawned. "Anything I can help you with?"

The leader reddened slightly.

"I am the commander of this sector!" he barked. "I demand to see Skeeve, commander of the defense, not his lacky!"

I dropped one of the bags of flash powder on the ground at my feet.

"If you insist," Aahz growled, "I'll get him. But he won't be happy."

"I'm not here to make him happy," the leader shouted. "Now be off with you."

"That won't be necessary," Aahz leered. "He's a magician. He hears and sees what his servants hear and see. He'll be along."

That was my cue. I let drop the sheet of invisibility and simultaneously ignited the bag of flash powder.

The results were spectacular.

The soldiers, with the exception of the leader, fell back several steps. To them, it looked as if I had suddenly appeared from thin air, materializing in a cloud of red smoke.

For me, the effect was less impressive. As the bag of flash powder went off, it was made apparent to me that watching a cloud of smoke from a distance was markedly different from standing at ground zero.

As I was enveloped in the scarlet billows, my feel-

ing was not of elated triumph but rather a nearly
overwhelming desire to cough and sneeze.

My efforts to suppress my reactions caused me to
contort my features to the point where I must have
borne more than a faint resemblance to Gus.

"Steady, Master!" Aahz cautioned.

"Aahz. Ah!" I gasped.

"Do not let your anger overcome your reason,"
my mentor continued hastily. "They don't know the
powers they trifle with."

"I . . . I did not wish to be disturbed," I managed
at last, regaining my breath as the smoke dissipated.

The leader of the group had held his ground
through the entire proceedings, though he looked a
bit paler and less sure of himself than when he had
been dealing with just Aahz.

"We . . . um . . . apologize for bothering you," he
began uncertainly. "But there are certain matters requiring your immediate attention . . . specifically the
war we are currently engaged in."

I eyed him carefully. He seemed to be of a different cut than Claude had been.

"I'm afraid you have me at a disadvantage, sir," I
said cagily. "You seem to know me, but I don't recall
having met you before."

"We have not met before," the officer replied
grimly. "If we had, be assured one of us would not
be here currently. I know you by reputation, specifically for your recent efforts to resist the advance of
our army. For myself, I am Antonio, commander of
the right wing of the left flank of the Empire's army.
These are my officers."

He indicated the soldiers behind him with a vague
wave of his hand. The men responded by drawing

themselves more erect and thrusting out their chins arrogantly.

I acknowledged them with a slight nod.

"Where is Claude?" I asked casually. "I was under the impression he was an officer of this sector."

"You are correct," Antonio smirked. "He *was*. He is currently being detained until he can be properly court-martialed . . . for incompetence!"

"Incompetence?" I echoed. "Come now, sir. Aren't you being a little harsh? While Claude may have overstepped his abilities a bit, I wouldn't say he's incompetent. I mean, after all, he *was* dealing with supernatural powers, if you know what I mean."

As I spoke, I wiggled my fingers dramatically at Aahz and removed his disguise.

The jaws of the attending officers dropped, ruining their arrogant jut. Then Aahz grinned at them, and their mouths clicked shut in unison as they swallowed hard.

Antonio was unimpressed.

"Yes, yes," he said briskly, waving a hand as if at an annoying fly. "We have had reports, many reports, as to your rapport with demons. Claude's incompetence is in his disastrous underestimation of the forces opposing him. Be assured, I will not be guilty of the same error."

"Don't count on it, Tony," Aahz leered. "We demons can be a pretty tricky lot.

The officer ignored him.

"However, we are not here for idle pleasantries," he said, fixing me with a stern gaze. "I believe we have a dispute to settle concerning right of passage over this particular piece of terrain."

"We have a dispute concerning your right of passage over the kingdom of Possiltum," I corrected.

"Yes, yes," Antonio yawned. "Of course, if you want to stop us from gaining Possiltum, you had best stop us here."

"That's about how we had it figured," Aahz agreed.

"Not to belabor the point, Antonio," I smiled, "but I believe we *do* have you stopped."

"Temporarily," the officer smiled. "I expect that situation to change shortly . . . shall we say, a few hours after dawn? Tomorrow?"

"We'll be here," Aahz nodded.

"Just a moment," I interrupted. "Antonio, you strike me as being a sporting man. Would you like to make our encounter tomorrow a little more interesting? Say, with a little side wager?"

"Such as what?" the officer scowled.

"If you lose tomorrow," I said carefully, "will you admit Claude's defeat had nothing to do with incompetence and drop the charges against him?"

Antonio thought for a moment, then nodded.

"Done," he said. "Normally I would fear what the reaction of my superiors would be, but I am confident of my victory. There are things even a demon cannot stand against."

"Such as?" Aahz drawled.

"You will see," the officer smiled. "Tomorrow."

With that, he spun on his heel and marched off, his officers trailing behind him.

"What do you think, Aahz?" I murmured.

"Think?" my mentor scowled. "I think you're

going soft, kid. First Brockhurst, now Claude. What is this 'be kind to enemies' kick you're on?"

"I meant about tomorrow," I clarified quickly.

"I dunno, kid," Aahz admitted. "He sounded too confident for comfort. I wish I knew what he's got up his sleeve that's supposed to stop demons."

"Well," I sighed, "I guess we'll see tomorrow."

Chapter
Twenty-One:

"It takes a giant to fight a giant."
—H. PRYM

OUR pensiveness was still with us the next day.

Our opponents were definitely up to something, but we couldn't tell exactly what it was. Tanda and Brockhurst had headed out on a scouting trip during the night and had brought back puzzling news. The Empire's soldiers had brought up some kind of heavy equipment, but it was hidden from sight by a huge box. All our scouts could say for sure was that whatever the secret weapon was, it was big and it was heavy.

Gus offered to fly over the box to take a quick peek inside, but we vetoed the idea. With the box constantly in the center of a mass of soldiers, there was no way the gargoyle could carry out his mission unobserved. Even if he used the invisibility sheet, the army was so far flung that someone would see him. So far we had kept the gargoyle's presence on our team as a secret, and we preferred to keep it that way. Even if we disguised him as Aahz or myself, it would betray the fact that someone in our party was able to fly. As Aahz pointed out, it looked as if this campaign would be rough enough without giving the opposition advance warning of the extent of our abilities.

This was all tactically sound and irrefutably logical. Nonetheless, it did nothing to reassure me as Aahz and I stood waiting for Antonio to make his opening gambit.

"Relax, kid," Aahz murmured. "You look nervous."

"I *am* nervous," I snapped back. "We're standing out here waiting to fight, and we don't know who or what we're supposed to be fighting. You'll forgive me if that makes me a trifle edgy."

I was aware I was being unnecessarily harsh on my mentor. Ajax and Gus were standing by, and Brockhurst and Tanda were watching for any new developments. The only team member unaccounted for this morning was the Gremlin, but I thought it wisest not to bring this to Aahz's attention. I assumed our elusive blue friend was off somewhere with Gleep, as my pet was also missing.

Everything that could have been done in preparation had been done. However, I still felt uneasy.

"Look at it this way, kid," Aahz tried again. "At least we know what we *aren't* up against."

What we weren't dealing with was soldiers. Though a large number of them were gathered in the near vicinity, there seemed to be no effort being made to organize or arm them for battle. As the appointed time drew near, it became more and more apparent that they were to be spectators only in the upcoming fray.

"I think I'd rather deal with soldiers," I said glumly.

"Heads up, kid," Aahz retorted, nudging me with his elbow. "Whatever's going to happen is about to."

I knew what he meant, which bothered me. There was no time to ponder it, however. Antonio had just put in his appearance.

He strolled around one corner of the mammoth box deep in conversation with a suspicious-looking character in a hooded cloak. He shot a glance in our direction, smiled, and waved merrily.

We didn't wave back.

"I don't like the looks of this, kid," Aahz growled.

I didn't either, but there wasn't much we could do except wait. Antonio finished his conversation with the stranger and stepped back, folding his arms across his chest. The stranger waved some of the onlooking soldiers aside, then stepped back himself. Drawing himself up, he began weaving his hands back and forth in a puzzling manner. Then the wind carried the sound to me and I realized he was chanting.

"Aahz!" I gasped. "They've got their own magician."

"I know," Aahz grinned back. "But from what I can hear he's bluffing them the same way you bluffed the court back at Possiltum. He probably doesn't have any more powers than I do."

No sooner had my mentor made his observation than the side of the huge box which was facing us

slowly lowered itself to the ground. Revealed inside
the massive container was a dragon.

The box had been big, better than thirty feet long
and twenty feet high, but from the look of the dragon
he must have been cramped for space inside.

He was big! I mean, really big!

Now I've never kidded myself about Gleep's size.
Though his ten-foot length might look big here on
Klah, I had seen dragons on Deva that made him
look small. The dragon currently facing us, however,
dwarfed everything I had seen before.

He was an iridescent bluish-green his entire length,
which was far more serpentine than I was accustomed to seeing in a dragon. He had massive bat
wings that he stretched and flexed as he clawed his
way out of the confining box. There was a silver glint
from his eye sockets which would have made him
look machinelike were it not for the fluid grace of his
powerful limbs.

For a moment, I was almost overcome by the
beautiful spectacle he presented, emerging onto the
battlefield. Then he threw his head back and roared,
and my admiration turned icy cold within me.

The great head turned until its eyes were focused
directly on us. Then he began to stalk forward.

"Time for the better part of valor, kid," Aahz
whispered, tugging at my sleeve. "Let's get out of
here."

"Wait a minute, Aahz!" I shot back. "Do you see
that? What the keeper's holding?"

A glint of gold in the sunlight had caught my eye.
The dragon's keeper had a gold pendant clasped in
his fist as he urged his beast forward.

"Yeah!" Aahz answered. "So?"

"I've seen a pendant like that before!" I explained excitedly. "That's how he's controlling the dragon!"

The Deveel who had been running the Dragon stall where I acquired Gleep had worn a pendant like that. The pendant was used to control dragons . . . unattached dragons, that is. Attached dragons can be controlled by their owner without other assistance. A dragon becomes attached to you when you feed it. That's how I got Gleep. I fed him, sort of. Actually, he helped himself to a hefty bit of my sleeve.

"Well, don't just stand there, kid," Aahz barked, interrupting my reverie. "Get it!"

I reached out with my mind and took a grab at the pendant. The keeper felt it start to go and tightened his grip on it, fighting me for its possession.

"I . . . I can't get it, Aahz," I cried. "He won't let go."

"Then hightail it outta here, kid," my mentor ordered. "Tell Ajax to bag us that keeper. Better tell Gus to stand by with Berfert just in case. I'll try to keep the dragon busy."

An image flashed in my mind. It was a view of me, Skeeve, court magician, bolting for safety while Aahz faced the dragon alone. Something snapped in my mind.

"You go!" I snapped.

"Kid, are you—"

"It's my war and my job," I shouted. "Now get going."

With that I turned to face the oncoming dragon, not knowing or caring if Aahz followed my orders. I was Skeeve!

But it was an awfully big dragon!

I tried again for the pendant, nearly lifting the

keeper from his feet with my effort, but the man clung firmly to his possession, screaming orders at the dragon as he did.

I shot a nervous glance at the grim behemoth bearing down on me. If I tried to levitate out of the way, he could just. . . .

"Look out, kid!" came Aahz's voice from behind me.

I half turned, then something barreled past me, positioning itself between me and the oncoming menace.

It was Gleep!

"Gleep!" I shouted. "Get back here!"

My pet paid me no mind. His master was being threatened, and he meant to have a hand in this no matter what I said.

No longer a docile, playful companion, he planted himself between me and the monster, lowered his head to the ground, and hissed savagely, a six-foot tongue of flame leaping from his mouth as he did.

The effect on the big dragon was astonishing. He lurched to a stop and sat back on his haunches, cocking his head curiously at the mini-dragon blocking his path.

Gleep was not content with stopping his opponent, however. Heedless of the fact that the other dragon was over four times his size he began to advance stiffly, challenging his rival's right to the field.

The large dragon blinked, then shot a look behind him. Then he looked down on Gleep again, drawing his head back until his long neck formed a huge question mark.

Gleep continued to advance.

I couldn't understand it. Even if the monster

couldn't flame, which was doubtful, it was obvious he had the sheer physical power to crush my pet with minimal effort. Still he did nothing, looking desperately about him almost as if he were embarrassed.

I watched in spellbound horror. It couldn't last. If nothing else, Gleep was getting too close to the giant to be ignored. Any minute now, the monster would have to react.

Finally, after a final glance at his frantic keeper, the big dragon did react. With a sigh, one of his taloned front paws lashed out horizontally in a cuff that would have caved in a building. It struck Gleep on the side of his head and sent him sprawling.

My pet was game, though, and struggled painfully to his feet, shaking his head as if to clear it.

Before he could assume his aggressive stance, however, the big dragon stretched his neck down until their heads were side by side, and he began to mutter and grumble in Gleep's ear. My dragon cocked his head as if listening, then "whuffed" in response.

As the stunned humans and nonhumans watched, the two dragons conversed in the center of the battlefield punctuating their mutterings with occasional puffs of smoke.

I tried to edge forward to get a better idea of exactly what was going on, but the big dragon turned a baleful eye on me and let loose a blast of flame which kept me at a respectful distance. Not that I was afraid, mind you; Gleep seemed to have the situation well in hand . . . or talon as the case might be. Well, I had always told Aahz that Gleep was a very talon-ted dragon.

Finally, the big dragon drew himself up, turned, and majestically left the field without a backward glance, his head impressively high. Ignoring the angry shouts of the soldiers, he returned to his box and dropped his haunches, sitting with his back to the entire proceeding.

His keeper's rage was surpassed only by Antonio's. He screamed at the keeper with purpled face and frantic gestures until the keeper angrily pulled the control pendant from around his neck, handed it to the officer, and stalked off. Antonio blinked at the pendant, then flung it to the ground and started off after the keeper.

That was all the opening I needed. Reaching out with my mind, I brought the pendant winging to my hand.

"Aahz!" I began.

"I don't believe it," my mentor mumbled to himself. "I saw it, but I still don't believe it."

"Gleep!"

My pet came racing up to my side, understandably pleased with himself.

"Hi, fella!" I cried, ignoring his breath and throwing my arms around his neck in a hug. "What happened out there, anyway?"

"Gleep!" my pet said evasively, carefully studying a cloud.

If I had expected an answer, it was clear I wasn't going to get one.

"I still don't believe it," Aahz repeated.

"Look, Aahz," I said, holding the pendant aloft. "Now we don't have to worry about that or any other dragon. We've shown a profit!"

"So we did," Aahz scowled. "But do me a favor, huh, kid?"

"What's that, Aahz?" I asked.

"If that dragon, or any dragon, wanders into our camp, don't feed it! We already have one, and that's about all my nerves can stand. Okay?"

"Sure, Aahz," I smiled.

"Gleep!" said my pet, rubbing against me for more petting, which he got.

Chapter
Twenty-Two:

"Hell hath no fury like a demon scorched."
—C. MATHER

OUR next war council made the previous ones look small. This was only to be expected, as we were dealing with the commander of the entire left flank of the Empire's army.

Our meeting was taking place in a pavilion constructed specifically for that purpose, and the structure was packed with officers, including Claude. It seemed Antonio was true to his word, even though he himself was not currently present.

In the face of such a gathering, we had decided to show a bit more force ourselves. To that end, Tanda and Brockhurst were accompanying us, while Gleep snuffled around outside. Gus and Ajax we were still holding in reserve, while the Gremlin had not reappeared since the confrontation of dragons.

I didn't like the officer we were currently dealing with. There was something about his easy, oily manner that set me on edge. I strongly suspected he had ascended to his current position by poisoning his rivals.

"So you'd like us to surrender," he was saying thoughtfully, drumming his fingers on the table before him.

". . . or withdraw, or turn aside," I corrected. "Frankly, we don't care what you do, as long as you leave Possiltum alone."

"We've actually been considering doing just that," the commander said, leaning back in his chair to study the pavilion's canopy.

"Is that why you've been moving up additional troops all day long?" Brockhurst asked sarcastically.

"Merely an internal matter, I assure you," the commander purred. "All my officers are assembled here, and they're afraid their troops will fall to mischief if left to their own devices."

"What my colleague means," Aahz interjected, "is we find it hard to believe you're actually planning to accede to our demands."

"Why not?" the commander shrugged. "That *is* what you've been fighting for, isn't it? There comes a point when a commander must ask himself if it won't cost him more dearly to fight a battle than to pass it by. So far, your resistance utilizing demons and dragons has shown us this battle could be difficult indeed."

"There are more where they come from," I interjected, "should the need arise."

"So you've demonstrated," the commander smiled, waving a casual hand at Tanda and Brockhurst. "Witches and devils made an impressive addition to your force."

I deemed it unwise to point out to him that Brockhurst was an Imp, not a Deveel.

"Then you agree to bypass Possiltum?" Aahz asked bluntly.

"I agree to discuss it with my officers," the commander clarified. "All I ask is that you leave one of your . . . ah . . . assistants behind."

"What for?" I asked. I didn't like the way he was eyeing Tanda.

"To bring you word of our decision, of course," the commander shrugged. "None of my men would dare enter your camp, even granted a messenger's immunity."

There was a mocking tone to his voice I didn't like.

"I'll stay, Skeeve," Aahz volunteered.

I considered it. Aahz had demonstrated his ability to take care of himself time and time again. Still I didn't trust the commander.

"Only if you are willing to give us one of your officers in return as a hostage," I replied.

"I've already said none of—" the commander began.

"He need not enter our camp," I explained. "He can remain well outside our force, on the edge of the tree line in full view of your force. I will personally guarantee his safety."

The commander chewed his lip thoughtfully.

"Very well," he said. "Since you have shown an interest in his career, I will give you Claude to hold as a hostage."

The young officer paled but remained silent.

"Agreed," I said. "We will await your decision."

I nodded to my comrades, and they obediently began filing out of the pavilion. Claude hesitated, then joined the procession.

I wanted to tell Aahz to be careful but decided

against it. It wouldn't do to admit my partner's vulnerability in front of the commander. Instead, I nodded curtly to the officers and followed my comrades.

Tanda and Brockhurst were well on their way back to the treeline. Claude, on the other hand, was waiting for me as I emerged and fell in step beside me.

"While we have a moment," he said stiffly, "I would like to thank you for interceding in my behalf with my superiors."

"Don't mention it," I mumbled absently.

"No, really," he persisted. "Chivalry to an opponent is rarely seen these days. I think—"

"Look, Claude," I growled, "credit it to my warped sense of justice. I don't like you, and didn't when we first met, but that doesn't make you incompetent. Unpleasant, perhaps, but not incompetent."

I was harsher with him than I had intended to be, but I was worried about Aahz.

Finding himself thus rebuked, he sank into an uncomfortable silence which lasted almost until we reached the trees. Then he cleared his throat and tried again.

"Um . . . Skeeve?"

"Yeah?" I retorted curtly.

"I . . . um . . . what I was trying to say was that I am grateful and would repay your favor by any reasonable means at my disposal."

Despite my concern, his offer penetrated my mind as a potential opportunity.

"Would answering a few questions fall under the heading of 'reasonable'?" I asked casually.

"Depending upon the questions," he replied carefully. "I am still a soldier, and my code of conduct clearly states—"

"Tell you what," I interrupted. "I'll ask the questions, and you decide which ones are okay to answer. Fair enough?"

"So it would seem," he admitted.

"Okay," I began. "First question. Do you think the commander will actually bypass Possiltum?"

The officer avoided my eyes for a moment, then shook his head briskly.

"I should not answer that," he said, "but I will. I do not feel the commander is even considering it as a serious possibility, nor does any officer in that tent. He is known as 'the Brute,' even among his most loyal and seasoned troops. May I assure you he did not acquire that nickname by surrendering or capitulating while his force was still intact."

"Then why did he go through the motions of the meeting just now?" I queried.

"To gain time," Claude shrugged. "As your assistants noted, he is using the delay to mass his troops. The only code he adheres to is 'Victory at all costs.' In this case, it seems it is costing him his honor."

I thought about this for a moment before asking my next question.

"Claude," I said carefully, "you've faced us in battle, and you know your own army. If your prediction is correct and the Brute attacks in force, in your opinion, what are our chances of victory?"

"Nil," the officer replied quietly. "I know it may sound like enemy propaganda, but I ask you to believe my sincerity. Even with the additional forces you displayed this evening, if the Brute sets the legions in motion, they'll roll right over you. Were I in your position, I would take advantage of the cover of night to slip away, and not fear the stigma of cowardice. You're facing the mightiest army ever assembled. Against such a force there is no cowardice, only self-preservation.''

I believed him. The only question was what should I do with the advice.

"I thank you for your counsel," I said formally. "And will consider your words carefully. For now, if you will please remain here in the open as promised, I must consult with my troops.''

"One more thing," Claude said, laying a restraining hand on my arm. "If any harm befalls your assistant, the one you left at the meeting, I would ask that you remember I was here with you and had no part in it.''

"I will remember," I nodded, withdrawing my arm. "But if the Brute tries to lay a hand on Aahz, I'll wager he'll wish he hadn't.''

As I turned to seek out my team, I wished I felt as confident as I sounded.

Tanda came to me readily when I caught her eye and beckoned her away from the others.

"What is it, Skeeve?" she asked as we moved away into the shadows. "Are you worried about Aahz?''

I was, though I didn't want to admit it just yet. The night was almost gone with no signs of movement or activity from the pavilion. Still, I clung to my faith in Aahz. When that failed, I turned my mind to other exercises to distract it from fruitless worry.

"Aahz can take care of himself," I said gruffly.

"There's something else I wanted your opinion on."

"What's that?" she asked, cocking her head.

"As you know," I began pompously, "I am unable to see the disguise spells I cast. Though everyone else is fooled, as the originator of the spell, I still continue to see things in their true form."

"I didn't know that," she commented. "But continue."

"Well," I explained, "I was thinking that if we actually have to fight the army, we could use additional troops. I've got an idea, but I need you to tell me if it actually works."

"Okay," she nodded. "What is it?"

I started to resume my oration, then realized I was merely stalling. Instead, I closed my eyes and focused my mind on the small grove of trees ahead.

"Hey!" cried Tanda. "That's terrific."

I opened my eyes, being careful to maintain the spell.

"What do you see?" I asked nervously.

"A whole pack of demons . . . oops . . . I mean Perverts," she reported gaily. "Bristling with swords and spears. That's wild!"

It worked. I was correct when I guessed that my disguise spell could work on any living thing, not just men and beasts.

"I've never seen anything like it," Tanda marveled. "Can you make them move?"

"I don't know," I admitted. "I just—"

"Boss! Hey, Boss!" Brockhurst shouted, sprinting up to us. "Come quick! You'd better see this!"

"What is it?" I called, but the Imp had reversed his course and was headed for the tree line.

A sudden fear clutched at my heart.

"C'mon, Tanda," I growled and started off.

By the time we reached the tree line the whole team was assembled there, talking excitedly among themselves.

"What is it?" I barked, joining them.

The group fell silent, avoiding my eyes. Brockhurst lifted a hand and pointed across the meadow.

There, silhouetted against a huge bonfire was Aahz, hanging by his neck from a crude gallows. His body was limp and lifeless as he rotated slowly at the end of the rope. At his feet, a group of soldiers were gathered to witness the spectacle.

Relief flooded over me, and I began to giggle hysterically. Hanging! If only they know!

Alarm showed in the faces of my team as they studied my reaction in shocked silence.

"Don't worry!" I gasped. "He's okay!"

Early in my career with Aahz, I had learned that one doesn't kill demons by hanging them. Their neck muscles are too strong! They can hang all day without being any the worse for wear. I had, of course, learned this the hard way one day when we. . . .

"At least they have the decency to burn the body," Claude murmured from close beside me.

My laughter died in my throat.

"What?" I cried, spinning around.

Sure enough, the soldiers had cut down Aahz's "body" and were carrying it toward the bonfire with the obvious intention of throwing it in.

Fire! That was a different story. Fire was one of the things that could kill Aahz deader than. . . .

"Ajax!" I cried. "Quick! Stop them from—"

It was too late.

With a heave from the soldiers, Aahz arched into the roaring flames. There was a quick burst of light, then nothing.

Gone! Aahz!

I stood staring at the bonfire in disbelief. Shock numbed me to everything else as my mind reeled at the impact of my loss.

"Skeeve!" Tanda said in my ear, laying a hand on my shoulder.

"Leave me alone!" I croaked.

"But the army . . ."

She let the word trail off, but it made its impact. Slowly I became conscious of the world around me.

The legions, having given us our answer, were massing for battle. Drums boomed, heralding the rising sun as it reflected off the polished weapons arrayed to face us.

The army. They had done this!

With deliberate slowness I turned to face Claude. He recoiled in fear from my gaze.

"Remember!" he cried desperately. "I had nothing to—"

"I remember," I replied coldly. "And for that reason only I am letting you go. I would advise, however, that you choose a path to follow other than rejoining the army. I have tried to be gentle with them, but if they insist on having war, as I am Skeeve, we shall give it to them!"

Chapter Twenty-Three:

"What is this, a Chinese fire drill?"
— SUN TZU

I DIDN'T see where Claude went after I finished speaking with him, nor did I care. I was studying the opposing army with a new eye. Up to now I had been thinking defensively, planning for survival. Now I was thinking as the aggressor.

The legions were in tight block formations, arrayed some three or four blocks deep and perhaps fifteen blocks wide. Together they presented an awesome impression of power, an irresistible force that would never retreat.

That suited me fine. In fact, I wanted a little insurance that they would not retreat.

"Ajax!" I called without turning my head.

"Here, youngster!" the bowman replied from close beside me.

"Can Blackie send your arrows out beyond those formations?"

183

"I reckon so," he drawled.

"Very well," I said grimly. "The same drill as the first battle, only this time don't go for the wagons. I want a half circle of fire around their rear."

As before, the bowstring set up a rhythmic "thung" as the bowman began to lose shaft after shaft. This time, however, it seemed the arrows burst into flame more readily.

"Ease off, youngster," Ajax called. "Yer burnin' em up before they reach the ground."

He was right. Either I was standing directly on a force line, or my anger had intensified my energies. Whatever the reason, I found myself with an incredible amount of power at my disposal.

"Sorry, Ajax," I shouted, and diverted a portion of my mind away from the ignition point.

"Tanda!" I called. "Run back and get Gleep!"

"Right, Skeeve," came the reply.

I had a hunch my pet might come in handy before this brawl was done.

The front row of the army's formation was beginning to advance to the rhythmic pounding of drums. I ignored them.

"Brockhurst!"

"Here, boss!" the Imp responded, stepping to my side.

"Have you spotted the commander yet?"

"Not yet," came the bitter reply. "He's probably buried back in the middle of the formation somewhere."

"Well, climb a tree or something and see if you can pinpoint him," I ordered.

"Right, boss! When I see him, do you want me to go after him?"

"No!" I replied grimly. "Report back to me. I

want to handle him myself."

The front line was still advancing. I decided I'd better do something about it. With a sweep of my mind, I set fire to the meadow in front of the line's center. The blocks confronted by this barrier ground to a halt while the right and left wings continued their forward movement.

"Gleep!" came a familiar voice accompanied by an even more familiar blast of bad breath.

"We're back!" Tanda announced unnecessarily.

I ignored them and studied the situation. Plumes of white smoke rising from behind the Empire's formation indicated that Ajax was almost finished with his task. Soon, the army would find itself cut off from any retreat. It was time to start thinking about our attack. The first thing I needed was more information.

"Gus!" I said thoughtfully, "I want you to take a quick flight over their formations. See if you can find a spot to drop Berfert where he can do some proper damage."

"Right, boss," the gargoyle grunted, lumbering forward.

"Wait a minute," I said, a thought occurring to me. "Tanda, have you still got the invisibility sheet with you?"

"Right here!" she grinned.

"Good," I nodded. "Gus, take the sheet with you. Keep it in front of you as long as you can while you're checking them out. There's no sense drawing fire until you have to."

The gargoyle accepted the sheet with a shrug.

"If you say so, boss," he muttered. "But they can't do much to me."

"Use it anyway," I ordered. "Now get moving."

The gargoyle sprang heavily into the air and started across the meadow with slow sweeps of his massive wings. I found it hard to believe anything that big and made of stone could fly, but I was seeing it. Maybe he used levitation.

"All set, youngster," Ajax chortled, interrupting my thoughts. "Anything else I can do for ya?"

"Not just now, Ajax," I replied. "But stand by."

I was glad that portion of my concentration was free now. This next stunt was going to take all the energy I could muster.

I focused my mind on the grass in front of the advancing left wing. As testimony to the effectiveness of my efforts, that portion of the line ground to an immediate halt.

"Say!" Tanda breathed in genuine admiration. "That's neat."

The effect I was striving for was to have the grass form itself into an army of Imps, rising from the ground to confront the Empire's troops. I chose Imps this time instead of demons because Imps are shorter, therefore requiring less energy to maintain the illusion.

Whatever my efforts actually achieved, it was enough to have the soldiers react. After several shouted orders from their officers, the troops let fly a ragged barrage of javelins at the grass in front of them. The weapons, of course, had no effect on their phantom foe.

"Say, youngster," Ajax said, nudging me lightly. "You want me to do something about those jokers shootin' at our gargoyle?"

I turned slightly to check Gus's progress. The flying figure had passed over the center line troops, the ones my fire was holding in check. The soldiers could now see the figure behind the invisible sheet, and were reacting with enviable competence.

The archers in their formation were busy loosing their shafts at this strange figure that had suddenly appeared overhead, while their comrades did their best to reach the gargoyle with hurled javelins.

I saw all this at a glance. I also saw something else.

"Wait a minute, Ajax," I ordered. "Look at that!"

The various missiles loosed by the center line were falling to earth in the massed formations of the troops still awaiting commands. Needless to say, this was not well received, particularly as they were still unable to see the actual target of their advance force. To them, it must have appeared that by some magik or demonic possession, their allies had suddenly turned and fired on them.

Now a few blocks began to return the fire, ordering their own archers into action. Others responded by raising their shields and starting forward with drawn swords.

The result was utter chaos, as the center line troops tried to defend themselves from the attacks of their own reinforcements.

Mind you, I hadn't planned it this way, but I was quick to capitalize on the situation. If the presence of a gargoyle could cause this kind of turmoil, I thought it would be a good idea to up the ante a little.

With a quick brush of my mind, I altered Gus's appearance. Now they had a full-grown dragon hovering over their midst. The effect was spectacular.

I, however, did not allow myself the luxury of watching. I had learned something in this brief exchange, and I wanted to try it out.

I dissolved my Imp army, then reformed them, not in front of the troops, but in their midst!

This threw the formations into total disorder. As the soldiers struck or threw at the phantom figures, more often than not they struck their comrades instead.

If this kept up, they would be too busy fighting each other to bother with us.

"Boss!" Brockhurst called, darting up to my side. "I've got the commander spotted!"

"Where?" I asked grimly, trying not to take my concentration from the battle raging in the meadow.

The Imp pointed.

Sure enough! There was the Brute, striding angrily from formation to formation, trying to restore order to his force.

I heard the telltale whisper of an arrow being drawn.

"Ajax!" I barked. "Hold your fire. He's mine . . . all mine!"

As I said this, I dissolved all the Imps in the Brute's vicinity, and instead changed the commander's features until he took on the appearance of Aahz.

The dazed soldiers saw a demon appear in their midst brandishing a sword, a demon of a type they knew could be killed. They needed no further prompting.

I had one brief glimpse of the Brute's startled face before his troops closed on him, then a forest of uniforms blotted him from my view.

"Mission accomplished, boss!" Gus announced, appearing beside me. "What next?"

"What . . . did you . . ." I stammered.

I had forgotten that on his return trip, the invisibility sheet would shield the gargoyle from our view. His sudden appearance had startled me.

"Berfert'll be along when he gets done with their siege equipment," Gus continued, waving toward the enemy.

I looked across the meadow. He was right! The heavy equipment which had been lined up behind the army was now in flames.

Then I noticed something else.

The army wasn't fighting each other anymore. I realized with a start that between settling accounts with the Brute and Gus's reappearance, I had forgotten to maintain the Imp army!

In the absence of any visible foe, the Empire troops had apparently come to their senses and were now milling about trying to reestablish their formations.

Soon now, they would be ready to attack again.

"What do we do next, boss?" Brockhurst asked eagerly.

That was a good question. I decided to stall while I tried to work out an answer.

"I'll draw you a diagram," I said confidently. "Somebody give me a sword."

"Here, kid. Use mine," Aahz replied, passing me the weapon.

"Thanks," I said absently. "Now, this line is their main formation. If we . . . *Aahz!?*"

"Ready and able," my mentor grinned. "Sorry I'm late."

It *was* Aahz! He was standing there calmly with his arms folded as if he had been part of our group all along. The reactions of the others, however, showed that they were as surprised as I was at his appearance.

"But you . . ." I stammered. "The fire . . ."

"Oh, that," Aahz shrugged. "About the time I figured what they were doing, I used the D-Hopper to blink out to another dimension. The only trouble was I hadn't gotten around to relabeling the controls yet, and I had a heck of a time finding my way back to Klah."

Relief flooded over me like a cool wave. Aahz was alive! More important, he was here! The prospects for the battle suddenly looked much better.

"What should we do next, Aahz?" I asked eagerly.

"I don't know why you're asking me," my mentor blinked innocently. "It looks like you've been doing a fine job so far all by yourself."

Terrific! Now that I need advice, I get compliments.

"Look, Aahz," I began sternly. "We've got a battle coming up that—"

"Boss!" Brockhurst interrupted. "Something's going on out there!"

With a sinking heart, I turned and surveyed the situation again.

A new figure had appeared on the scene, an officer from the look of him. He was striding briskly along the front of the formation alternately shouting and waving his hands. Trailing along in his wake was a cluster of officers, mumbling together and shaking their hands.

"What in the world is that all about?" I murmured half to myself.

"Brace yourself, kid," Aahz advised. "If I'm hearing correctly, it's bad news."

"C'mon, Aahz," I sighed. "How could things get worse than they already are?"

"Easy," Aahz retorted. "*That* is the supreme commander of the Empire's army. He's here to find out what's holding up his left flank's advance."

Chapter
Twenty-Four:

*" . . . and then I said to myself, 'Why
should I split it two ways—'"*
—G. MOUSER

THE supreme commander's name was Big Julie, and
he was completely different from what I had expected.

For one thing, when he called for a war council,
he came to us. Flanked by his entire entourage of
officers, he came all the way across the meadow to
stand just short of the tree line, and he came unarmed. What was more, all of his officers were
unarmed, presumably at his insistence.

He seemed utterly lacking in the arrogance so
prevalent in the other officers we had dealt with, in-
viting us into the large tent he had had erected in the
meadow for the meeting. Introducing him to the
members of my force, I noticed he treated them with
great respect and seemed genuinely pleased to meet
each of them, even Gleep.

Our whole team was present for the meeting. We

figured that if there was ever a time to display our power, this was it.

In a surprising show of generosity, Aahz broke out the wine and served drinks to the assemblage. I was a little suspicious of this. Aahz isn't above doctoring drinks to win a fight, but when I caught his eye and raised an eyebrow, he responded with a small shake of his head. Apparently he was playing this round straight.

Then we got down to business.

Big Julie heard us out, listening with rapt attention. When we finished, he sighed and shook his head.

"Ah'm sorry," he announced. "But I can't do it. We've got to keep advancing, you know? That's what armies do!"

"Couldn't you advance in another direction for a while?" I suggested hopefully.

"Aie!" he exclaimed, spreading his hands defensively. "What do you think I got here, geniuses? These are soldiers. They move in straight lines, know what I mean?"

"Do they have to move so vigorously?" Aahz muttered. "They don't leave much behind."

"What can I say?" Big Julie shrugged. "They're good boys. They do their job. Sometimes they get a little carried away . . . like the Brute."

I had hoped to avoid the subject of the Brute, but since it had come up, I decided to face it head on.

"Say . . . um . . . Julie," I began.

"Big Julie!" one of the officers growled out of the corner of his mouth.

"Big Julie!" I amended hastily. "About the Brute. Um . . . he was . . . well . . . I wanted . . ."

"Don't mention it," Julie waved. "You want to

know the truth? You did me a favor.''

"I did?'' I blinked.

"I was getting a little worried about the Brute, you know what I mean?'' the commander raised his eyebrows. "He was getting a little too ambitious.''

"In that case. . . .'' I smiled.

"Still . . .'' Julie continued, "that's a bad way to go. Hacked apart by your own men. I wouldn't want that to happen to me.''

"You should have fed him to the dragons,'' Aahz said bluntly.

"The Brute?'' Julie frowned. "Fed to the dragons? Why?''

"Because then he could have been 'et, too'!''

Apparently this was supposed to be funny, as Aahz erupted into sudden laughter as he frequently does at his own jokes. Tanda rolled her eyes in exasperation.

Big Julie looked vaguely puzzled. He glanced at me, and I shrugged to show I didn't know what was going on either.

"He's strange,'' Julie announced, stabbing an accusing finger at Aahz. "What's a nice boy like you doing hanging around with strange people? Hey?''

"It's the war,'' I said apologetically. "You know what they say about strange bedfellows.''

"You seem to be doin' all right for yourself!'' Julie winked, then leered at Tanda.

"You want I should clean up his act, Boss?'' Brockhurst asked grimly, stepping forward.

"See!'' Julie exploded. "That's what I mean. This is no way to learn warfare. Tell you what. Why don't you let me fix you up with a job, hey? What do you say to that?''

"What pay scale?'' Aahz asked.

"Aahz!" I scowled, then turned back to Julie. "Sorry, but we've already got a job . . . defending Possiltum. I appreciate your offer, but I don't want to leave a job unfinished."

"What have I been telling you?" Julie appealed to his officers. "All the good material has been taken already. Why can't you bring me recruits like this, eh?"

This was all very flattering, but I clung tenaciously to the purpose of our meeting.

"Um . . . Jul . . . I mean, Big Julie," I continued. "About defending Possiltum. Couldn't you find another kingdom somewhere to attack? We really don't want to have to fight you."

"*You* don't want to fight?" Julie erupted sarcastically. "You think *I* want to fight? You think I *like* doing this for a living? You think my boys like killing and conquering all the time?"

"Well . . ." I began tactfully.

Big Julie wasn't listening. He was out of his seat and pacing up and down, gesturing violently to emphasize his words.

"What kind of ding-bat *wants* to fight?" he asked rhetorically. "Do I look crazy? Do my boys look crazy? Everybody thinks we got some kind of weird drive that keeps us going. They think that all we want to do in the whole world is march around in sweaty armor and sharpen swords on other people's helmets. That's what you think too, isn't it? Eh? Isn't it?"

This last was shouted directly at me. By now I was pretty fed up with being shouted at.

"Yes!" I roared angrily. "That's what I think!"

"Well," Julie scowled. "You're wrong because—"

"That's what I think because if you didn't like doing it, you wouldn't do it!" I continued, rising to my own feet.

"Just like that!" Julie shouted sarcastically. "Just stop and walk away."

He turned and addressed his officers.

"He thinks it's easy! Do you hear *that?* Any of you who don't like to fight, just stop. Eh? Just like that."

A low chorus of chuckles rose from his assembled men. Despite my earlier burst of anger, I found myself starting to believe him. Incredible as it seemed, Julie and his men didn't like being soldiers!

"You think we wouldn't quit if we could?" Julie was saying to me again. "I bet there isn't a man in my whole army who wouldn't take a walk if he thought he could get away with it."

Again there was a murmur of assent from his officers.

"I don't understand," I said, shaking my head. "If you don't want to fight, and we don't want to fight, what are we doing here?"

"Did you ever hear of loan sharks?" Julie asked. "You know about organized crime?"

"Organized crime?" I blinked.

"It's like government, kid," Aahz supplied. "Only more effective."

"You'd better believe 'more effective,' " Julie nodded. "That's what we're doing here! Me and the boys, we got a list of gambling debts like you wouldn't believe. We're kinda working it off, paying 'em back in land, you know what I mean?"

"You haven't answered my question," I pointed out. "Why don't you just quit?"

"Quit?" Julie seemed genuinely astonished. "You

gotta be kidding. If I quit before I'm paid up, they break my leg. You know?'' His wolfish grin left no doubt the thugs in question would do something a great deal more fatal and painful than just breaking a leg.

''It's the same with the boys here. Right, boys?'' He indicated his officers with a wave of his hand.

Vigorous nods answered his wave.

''And you ought to see the collection agent they use. Kid, you might be a fair magician where you come from. But''—he shuddered—''this, believe me, you don't want to see.''

Knowing how tough Big Julie was, I believed him.

Giving me a warm smile, he draped his arm around my shoulders.

''That's why it's really gonna break my heart to kill you. Ya know?''

''Well,'' I began, ''you don't have to . . . KILL ME?''

''That's right,'' he nodded vigorously. ''I knew you'd understand. A job's a job, even when you hate it.''

''Whoa!'' Aahz interrupted, holding one flattened hand across the top of the other to form a crude T. ''Hold it! Aren't you overlooking something, Jules?''

''That's 'Big Julie.' '' one of the guards admonished.

''I don't care if he calls himself the Easter Bunny!'' my mentor snarled. ''He's still overlooking something.''

''What's that?'' Julie asked.

''Us.'' Aahz smiled, gesturing to the team. ''Aside from the minor detail that Skeeve here's a magician and not that easy to kill, he's got friends. What do you think we'll be doing while you make a try for our leader?''

The whole team edged forward a little. None of them were smiling, not even Gus. Even though they were my friends who I knew and loved, I had to admit they looked mean. I was suddenly very glad they were on my side.

Big Julie, on the other hand, seemed unimpressed.

"As a matter of fact," he smiled, "I expect you to be dying right along with your leader. That is, unless you're really good at running."

"Running from what?" Gus growled. "I still think you're overlooking something. By my count, we've got you outnumbered. Even if you were armed—"

The supreme commander cut him short with a laugh. It was a relaxed, confident laugh which no one else joined in on. Then the laugh disappeared, and he leaned forward with a fierce scowl.

"Now, I'm only gonna say this once, so alla you listen close. Big Julie didn't get where he is today by overlooking nothin'. You think I'm outnumbered? Well, maybe you'd just better count again."

Without taking his eyes from us, he waved his hand in a short, abrupt motion. At the signal, one of his guards pulled a cord and the sides of the tent fell away.

There were soldiers outside. They hadn't been there when we entered the tent, but they were there now. Hoo boy were they. Ranks and ranks of them completely surrounding the tent, the nearest barely an arm's length away. The front three rows were archers, with arrows nocked and drawn, leveled at our team.

I realized with a sudden calm clarity that I was

about to die. The whole meeting had been a trap, and it was a good one. Good enough that we would all be dead if we so much as twitched. I couldn't even kid myself that I could stop that many arrows if they were all loosed at once. Gus might survive the barrage, and maybe the others could blip away to another dimension in time to save themselves, but I was too far away from Aahz and the D-Hopper to escape.

"I . . . um . . . thought war councils were supposed to be off limits for combat." I said carefully.

"I also didn't get where I am today by playing fair," Big Julie shrugged.

"You know," Aahz drawled, "for a guy who doesn't want to fight, you run a pretty nasty war."

"What can I say?" the supreme commander asked, spreading his hands in helpless appeal. "It's a job. Believe me, if there was any other way, I'd take it. But as it is . . ."

His voice trailed off, and he began to raise his arm. I realized with horror that when his hand came down, so would the curtain.

"How much time do we have to find another way?" I asked desperately.

"You don't," Big Julie sighed.

"AND WE DON'T NEED ANY!" Aahz roared with sudden glee.

All eyes turned toward him, including my own. He was grinning broadly while listening to something the Gremlin was whispering in his ear.

"What's that supposed to mean?" the supreme commander demanded. "And where did this little blue fella come from? Eh?"

He glared at the encircling troops, who looked at

each other in embarrassed confusion.

"This is a Gremlin," Aahz informed him, slipping a comradely arm around the shoulders of his confidant, "And I think he's got the answer to our problems. *All* our problems. You know what I mean?"

"What does he mean?" Julie scowled at me. "Do you understand what he's sayin'?"

"Tell him, Aahz," I ordered confidently, wondering all the while what possible solution my mentor could have found to this mess.

"Big Julie," Aahz smiled, "what could those loan sharks of yours do if you and your army simply disappeared?"

And so, incredibly, it was ended.

Not with fireworks or an explosion or a battle. But like a lot of things in my life, in as crazy and off-hand a way as it had started.

And when it had ended, I almost wished it hadn't.

Because then I had to say good-bye to the team.

Saying good-bye to the team was harder than I would have imagined. Somehow, in all my planning, I had never stopped to consider the possibility of emerging victorious from the war.

Despite my original worries about the team, I found I had grown quite close to each of them. I would have liked to keep them around a little longer, but that would have been impossible. Our next stop was the capital, and they would be a little too much to explain away.

Besides, as Aahz pointed out, it was bad for morale to let the troops find out how much their commander was being paid, particularly when it was extremely disproportionate to their own wages.

Following his advice, I paid each of them personally. When I was done, however, I found myself strangely at a loss for words. Once again, the team came to my aid.

"Well, boss," Brockhurst sighed. "I guess this is it. Thanks for everything."

"It's been a real pleasure working for you," Gus echoed. "The money's nice, but the way I figure it, Berfert and I owe you a little extra for getting us out of that slop chute. Anytime you need a favor, look us up."

"Youngster," Ajax said, clearing his throat, "I move around a lot, so I'm not that easy to track. If you ever find yourself in a spot where you think I can lend a hand, jes' send a message to the Bazaar and I'll be along shortly."

"I didn't think you visited the Bazaar that often," I asked, surprised.

"Normally I don't," the bowman admitted. "But I will now . . . jest in case."

Tanda was tossing her coin in the air and catching it with practiced ease.

"I shouldn't take this," she sighed. "But a girl's gotta eat."

"You earned it," I insisted.

"Yea, well, I guess we'll be going," she said, beckoning to the others. "Take care of yourself, handsome."

"You will be coming back?" I asked hurriedly.

She made a face.

"I don't think so," she said wryly, "If Grimble saw us together . . ."

"I meant, ever," I clarified.

She brightened immediately.

"Sure," she winked. "You won't get rid of me that easily. Say good-bye to Aahz for me."

"Say good-bye to him yourself," Aahz growled, stepping out of the shadows.

"There you are!" Tanda grinned. "Where's the Gremlin? I thought you two were talking."

"We were," Aahz confirmed, looking around him. "I don't understand. He was here a minute ago."

"It's as if he didn't exist, isn't it, Aahz?" I suggested innocently.

"Now look, kid!" my mentor began angrily.

A chorus of laughter erupted from the team. He spun in that direction to deliver a scathing reply, but there was a blip of light and they were gone.

We stood silently together for several moments staring at the vacant space. Then Aahz slipped an arm around my shoulder.

"They were a good team, kid," he sighed. "Now pull yourself together. Triumphant generals don't have slow leaks in the vicinity of their eyes. It's bad for the image."

Chapter
Twenty-Five:

"Is everybody happy?"

—MACHIAVELLI

AAHZ and I entered the capital at the head of a jubilant mob of Possiltum citizens.

We were practically herded to the front of the palace by the crowd pressing us forward. The cheering was incredible. Flowers and other less identifiable objects were thrown at us or strewn in our path, making the footing uncertain enough that more than once I was afraid of falling and being trampled. The people, at least, seemed thoroughly delighted to see us. All in all, though, our triumphal procession was almost as potentially injurious to our life and limb as the war had been.

I was loving it.

I had never had a large crowd make a fuss over me before. It was nice.

"Heads up, kid," Aahz murmured, nudging me in the ribs. "Here comes the reception committee."

Sure enough, there was another procession emerging from the main gates of the palace. It was smaller

than ours, but made up for what it lacked in numbers
with the prestige of its members.

The king was front and center, flanked closely by
Grimble and Badaxe. The chancellor was beaming
with undisguised delight. The general, on the other
hand, looked positively grim.

Sweeping the crowd with his eyes, Badaxe spotted
several of his soldiers in our entourage. His dark expression grew even darker, boding ill for those men. I
guessed he was curious as to why they had failed to
carry out his orders to stop our return.

Whatever he had in mind, it would have to wait.
The king was raising his arms, and the assemblage
obediently fell silent to hear what he had to say.

"Lord Magician," he began, "know that the
cheers of the grateful citizens of Possiltum only echo
my feelings for this service you have done us."

A fresh wave of applause answered him.

"News of your victory has spread before you," he
continued. "And already our historians are record-
ing the details of your triumph . . . as much as is
known, that is."

An appreciative ripple of laughter surged through
the crowd.

"While we do not pretend to comprehend the
workings of your powers," the king announced, "the
results speak for themselves. A mighty army of in-
vincible warriors vanished into thin air, weapons and
all. Only their armor and siege machines littering the
empty battlefield mark their passing. The war is won!
The threat to Possiltum is ended forever!"

At this, the crowd exploded. The air again filled
with flowers and shouting shook the very walls of the
palace.

The king tried to shout something more, but it was
lost in the jubilant noise. Finally he shrugged and

reentered the palace, pausing only for a final wave at the crowd.

I thought it was a rather cheap ploy, allowing him to cash in on our applause as if it were intended for him, but I let it go. Right now we had bigger fish to fry.

Catching the eyes of Grimble and Badaxe, I beckoned them forward.

"I've got to talk to you two," I shouted over the din.

"Shouldn't we go inside where it's quieter?" Grimble shouted back.

"We'll talk here!" I insisted.

"But the crowd . . ." the chancellor gestured.

I turned and nodded to a figure in the front row of the mob. He responded by raising his right arm in a signal. In response, the men in the forefront of the crowd locked arms and formed a circle around us, moving with near military precision. In a twinkling, there was a space cleared in the teeming populace, with the advisors, Aahz, Gleep, myself, and the man who had given the signal standing alone at its center.

"Just a moment," Badaxe rumbled, peering suspiciously at the circle. "What's going on—"

"General!" I beamed, flashing my biggest smile. "I'd like you to meet the newest citizen of Possiltum."

Holding my smile, I beckoned the mob leader forward.

"General Badaxe," I announced formally, "meet Big Julie. Big Julie, Hugh Badaxe!"

"Nice to meet you!" Julie smiled. "The boy here, he's been tellin' me all about you!"

The general blanched as he recognized the Empire's top commander.

"You!" he stammered. "But you . . . you're—"

"I hope you don't mind, General," I said smoothly. "But I've taken the liberty of offering Big Julie a job . . . as your military consultant."

"Military consultant?" Badaxe echoed suspiciously.

"What's the matter," Julie scowled. "Don't you think I can do it?"

"It's not that," the general clarified hastily. "It's just that . . . well—"

"One thing we neglected to mention, General," Aahz interrupted. "Big Julie here is retiring from active duty. He's more than willing to leave the running of Possiltum's army to you, and agrees to give advice only when asked."

"That's right!" Julie beamed. "I just wanna sit in the sun, drink a little wine, maybe pat a few bottoms, you know what I mean?"

"But the king . . ." Badaxe stammered.

". . . . doesn't have to be bothered with it at all," Aahz purred. "Unless, of course, you deem it necessary to tell him where your new battle plans are coming from."

"Hmm," the general said thoughtfully. "You sure you'd be happy with things that way, Julie?"

"Positive!" Julie nodded firmly. "I don't want any glory, no responsibility, and no credit. I had too much of that when I was workin' for the Empire, you know what I mean? Me and the boys talked it over, and we decided—"

"The boys?" Badaxe interrupted, frowning.

"Um . . . that's another thing we forgot to mention, General," I smiled. "Big Julie isn't the only new addition to Possiltum's citizenry."

I jerked my head at the circle of men holding back the crowd.

The general blinked at the men, then swiveled his

head around noting how many more like them were scattered through the crowd. He blanched as it became clear to him both where the Empire's army had disappeared to, and why his men had been unsuccessful in stopping our return to the capital.

"You mean to tell me you—" Badaxe began.

"Happy Possiltum citizens all, General!" Aahz proclaimed, then dropped his voice to a more confidential level. "I think you'll find that if you should ever have to draft an army, these new citizens will train a lot faster than your average plow pusher."

Apparently the general did. His eyes glittered at the thought of the new force we had placed at his command. I could see him mentally licking his chops in anticipation of the next war.

"Big Julie!" he declared with a broad smile. "You and your . . . er . . . boys are more than welcome to settle here in Possiltum. Let me be one of the first to congratulate you on your new citizenship."

He extended his hand, but there was an obstruction in his way. The obstruction's name was J.R. Grimble.

"Just a moment!" the chancellor snarled. "There's one minor flaw in your plans. It is my intention to advise the king to disband Possiltum's army."

"What?" roared Badaxe.

"Let me handle this, General," Aahz said soothingly. "Grimble, what would you want to do a fool thing like that for?"

"Why, because of the magician, of course," the chancellor blinked. "You've demonstrated he is quite capable of defending the kingdom without the aid of an army, so I see no reason why we should continue to bear the cost of maintaining one."

"Nonsense!" Aahz scolded. "Do you think the

great Skeeve has nothing to do with his time but guard your borders? Do you want to tie up your high-cost magician doing the job a low-cost soldier could do?"

"Well . . ." Grimble scowled.

"Besides," Aahz continued. "Skeeve will be spending considerable time on the road furthering his studies . . . which will of course increase his value to Possiltum. Who will guard your kingdom while he's away, if not the army?"

"But the cost is . . ." Grimble whined.

"If anything," Aahz continued ignoring the chancellor's protests. "I should think you'd want to expand your army now that your borders have increased in size."

"What's that?" Grimble blinked, "What about our borders?"

"I thought it was obvious," Aahz said innocently. "All these new citizens have to settle somewhere . . . and there is a lot of land up for grabs just north of here. As I understand it, it's completely unguarded at the moment. Possiltum wouldn't even have to fight for it, just move in and settle. That is, of course, provided you have a strong army to hold it once you've got it."

"Hmm," the chancellor said thoughtfully, stroking his chin with his hand.

"Then again," Aahz murmured quietly, "there's all the extra tax money the new citizens and land will contribute to the kingdom's coffers."

"Big Julie!" Grimble beamed. "I'd like to welcome you and your men to Possiltum."

"I'm welcoming him first!" Badaxe growled. "He's *my* advisor."

As he spoke, the general dropped his hand to the

hilt of his axe, a move which was not lost on the chancellor.

"Of course, General," Grimble acknowledged, forcing a grin. "I'll just wait here until you're through. There are a few things I want to discuss with our new citizens."

"While you're waiting, Grimble," Aahz smiled, "there are a few things we have to discuss with you."

"Such as what?" the chancellor scowled.

"Such as the Court Magician's pay!" my mentor retorted.

"Of course," Grimble laughed. "As soon as we're done here we'll go inside and I'll pay him his first month's wages."

"Actually," Aahz drawled. "What we wanted to discuss was an increase."

The chancellor stopped laughing.

"You mean a bonus, don't you?" he asked hopefully. "I'm sure we can work something out, considering—"

"I mean an increase!" Aahz corrected firmly. "C'mon, Grimble. The kingdom's bigger now. That means the magician's job is bigger and deserves more pay."

"I'm not sure I can approve that," the chancellor responded cagily.

"With the increase of your tax base," Aahz pressed, "I figure you can afford—"

"Now let's be careful," Grimble countered. "Our overhead has gone up right along with that increase. In fact, I wouldn't be surprised if . . ."

"C'mon, Gleep," I murmured to my pet. "Let's go see Buttercup."

I had a feeling the wage debate was going to last for a while.

Chapter
Twenty-Six:

"All's well that ends well."

—E. A. POE

I WAS spending a leisurely afternoon killing time in my immense room in the palace.

The bargaining session between Aahz and Grimble had gone well for us. Not only had I gotten a substantial wage increase, I was also now housed in a room which was only a little smaller than Grimble's, which in turn was second only to the king's in size. What was more, the room had a large window, which was nice even if it did look out over the stables. Aahz had insisted on this, hinting darkly that I might be receiving winged visitors in the night. I think this scared me more than it did Grimble, but I got my window.

When I chose, I could look down from my perch and keep an eye on Gleep and Buttercup in the stables. I could also watch the hapless stable boy who had been assigned to catering to their every need. That had been part of the deal, too, though I had pushed for it a lot harder than Aahz.

Aahz was housed in the adjoining room, which was nice, though smaller than mine. The royal architects were scheduled to open a door in our shared wall, and I had a hunch that when they did, the room arrangement would change drastically. For the moment, at least, I had a bit of unaccustomed privacy.

The room itself, however, was not what was currently commanding my attention. My mind was focused on Garkin's old brazier. I had been trying all afternoon to unlock its secrets, thus far without success. It stood firmly in the center of the floor where I had first placed it, stubbornly resisting my efforts.

I perched on my windowsill and studied the object glumly. I could levitate it easily enough, but that wasn't what I wanted. I wanted it to come alive and follow me around the way it used to follow Garkin.

That triggered an idea in my mind. It seemed silly, but nothing else had worked.

Drawing my eyebrows together, I addressed the brazier without focusing my energies on it.

"Come here!" I thought.

The brazier seemed to waiver for a moment, then it trotted to my side, clacking across the floor on its spindly legs.

It worked! Even though it was a silly little detail, the brazier's obedience somehow made me feel more like a magician.

"Hey, kid!" Aahz called, barging through my door without knocking. "Have you got a corkscrew?"

"What's a corkscrew?" I asked reflexively.

"Never mind," my mentor sighed. "I'll do it myself."

With that, he shifted the bottle of wine he was

holding to his left hand, and inserted the claw on his right forefinger into the cork. The cork made a soft pop as he gently eased it from the neck of the bottle, whereupon the cork was casually tossed into a corner as Aahz drank deeply of the wine.

"Ahh!" he gasped, coming up for air. "Terrific bouquet!"

"Um . . . Aahz?" I said shyly, leaving my window perch and moving to the table. "I have something to show you."

"First, could you answer a question?" Aahz asked.

"What?" I frowned.

"Why is that brazier following you around the room?"

I looked, and was startled to find he was right! The brazier had scuttled from the window to the table to remain by my side. The strange part was that I hadn't summoned it.

"Um . . . that's what I was going to show you," I admitted. "I've figured out how to get the brazier to come to me all by itself . . . no levitation or anything."

"Swell," Aahz grunted. "Now, can you make it stop?"

"Um . . . I don't know," I said, sitting down quickly in one of the chairs.

I didn't want to admit it, but while we were talking I had tried several mental commands to get the brazier to go away, all without noticeable effect. I'd have to work this out on my own once Aahz had left.

"Say, Aahz," I said casually, propping my feet on the table. "Could you pour me some of that wine?"

Aahz cocked an eyebrow at me, then crossed the

room slowly to stand by my side.

"Kid," he said gently, "I want you to look around real carefully. Do you see anybody here except you and me?"

"No," I admitted.

"Then we're in private, not in public . . . right?" he smiled.

"That's right," I agreed.

"Then get your own wine, apprentice!" he roared, kicking my chair out from under me.

Actually, it wasn't as bad as it sounds. I exerted my mind before I hit the floor and hovered safely in thin air. From that position, I reached out with my mind and lifted the bottle from Aahz's hand, transferring it to my own.

"If you insist," I said casually, taking a long pull on the bottle.

"Think you're pretty smart, don't you!" Aahz snarled, then he grinned. "Well, I guess you are at that. You've done pretty well . . . for an amateur."

"A professional," I corrected with a grin. "A salaried professional."

"I know." Aahz grinned back. "For an amateur, you're pretty smart. For a professional you've got a lot to learn."

"C'mon, Aahz!" I protested.

"But that can wait for another day," Aahz conceded. "You might as well relax for a while and enjoy yourself . . . while you can."

"What's that supposed to mean?" I frowned.

"Nothing!" Aahz shrugged innocently. "Nothing at all."

"Wait a minute, Aahz," I said sharply, regaining my feet. "I'm Court Magician now, right?"

"That's right, Skeeve," my mentor nodded.

"Court Magician is the job you pushed me into because it's so easy, right?" I pressed.

"Right again, kid." He smiled, his nodding becoming even more vigorous.

"Then nothing can go wrong? Nothing serious?" I asked anxiously.

Aahz retrieved his wine bottle and took a long swallow before answering.

"Just keep thinking that, kid." He grinned. "It'll help you sleep nights."

"C'mon, Aahz!" I whined. "You're supposed to be my teacher. If there's something I'm missing, you've got to tell me. Otherwise I won't learn."

"Very well, *apprentice*." Aahz smiled, evilly emphasizing the word. "There are a few things you've overlooked."

"Such as?" I asked, writhing under his smile.

"Such as Gus, Ajax, and Brockhurst, who you just sent back to Deva without instructions."

"Instructions?" I blinked.

"Tanda we don't have to worry about, but the other three—"

"Wait a minute, Aahz," I interrupted before he got too far from the subject. "What instructions?"

"Instructions not to talk about our little skirmish here," Aahz clarified absently. "Tanda will know enough to keep her mouth shut, but the others won't."

"You think they'll talk?"

"Is a frog's behind watertight?" Aahz retorted.

"What's a frog?" I countered.

"Money in their pockets, fresh from a successful campaign against overwhelming odds . . . of course they'll talk!'' Aahz thundered. "They'll talk their fool heads off to anyone who'll listen. What's more, they'll embellish it a little more with each telling until it sounds like they're the greatest fighters ever to spit teeth and you're the greatest tactician since Gronk!''

"What's wrong with that?'' I inquired, secretly pleased. I didn't know who Gronk was, but what Aahz was saying had a nice ring to it.

"Nothing at all.'' Aahz responded innocently. "Except now the word will be out as to who you are, where you are, and what you are . . . also that you're for hire and that you subcontract. If there's any place in all the dimensions that folks will take note of information like that, it's the Bazaar.''

Regardless of what my mentor may think, I'm not slow. I realized in a flash the implications of what he was saying . . . realized them and formulated an answer.

"So we suddenly get a lot of strange people dropping in on us to offer jobs, or looking for work,'' I acknowledged. "So what? All that means is I get a lot of practice saying 'No.' Who knows, it might improve my status around here a little if it's known that I regularly consult with strange beings from other worlds.''

"Of course,'' Aahz commented darkly, "there's always the chance that someone at the Bazaar will hear that the other side is thinking of hiring you and decide to forcibly remove you from the roster. Either that, or some young hotshot will want to make a name for himself by taking on this unbeatable magician everyone's talking about.''

I tried not to show how much his grim prophecy had unnerved me. Then I realized he would probably keep heaping it on until he saw me sweat. Consequently, I sweated . . . visibly.

"I hadn't thought of that, Aahz," I admitted. "I guess I did overlook something there."

"Then again there's Grimble and Badaxe," Aahz continued as if he hadn't heard me.

"What about Grimble and Badaxe?" I asked nervously.

"In my estimation," Aahz yawned, "the only way those two would ever work together would be against a common foe. In my further estimation, the best candidate for that 'common foe' position is you!"

"Me?" I asked in a very small voice.

"You work it out, kid," my mentor shrugged. "Until you hit the scene there was a two-way power struggle going as to who had the king's ear. Then you came along and not only saved the kingdom, you increased the population, expanded the borders, and added to the tax base. That makes you the most popular and therefore the most influential person in the king's court. Maybe I'm wrong, but I don't think Grimble and Badaxe are going to just sigh and accept that. It's my guess they'll 'double team' you and attack anything you say or do militarily and monetarily, and that's a tough one-two punch to counter."

"Okay. Okay. So there were two things I overlooked," I said. "Except for that—"

"And of course there's the people Big Julie and his men owe money to," Aahz commented thoughtfully. "I wonder how long it will be before they start nosing around looking for an explanation as to what happened to an entire army? More important, I wonder who they'll be looking for by name to provide them with that explanation?"

"Aahz?"

"Yeah, kid?"

"Do you mind if I have a little more of that wine?"

"Help yourself, kid. There's lots."

I had a hunch that was going to be the best news I would hear for a long time.